Shadows
and Sorrows

Also by Michael D. Graves

All Hallows' Shadows

2021 Kansas Notable Book
Midwest Book Award Finalist
J. Donald Coffin Memorial Book Award

Shadow of Death

To Leave a Shadow

2016 Kansas Notable Book

Green Bike, a group novel
with Kevin Rabas and Tracy Million Simmons

Shadows and Sorrows

by Michael D. Graves

Meadowlark Press, LLC
PO BOX 333, Emporia, KS 66801
Meadowlark-books.com

Cover photo by Dave Leiker
daveleikerphotography.com

FICTION / Mystery & Detective / Private Investigators
FICTION / Mystery & Detective / Historical
FICTION / Crime

Library of Congress Control Number: 2022931965

ISBN: 978-1-956578-03-4

*This is for my sons, Steve and David,
who let me coach them in the beginning. It didn't take them
long to outplay their coach, but I'm still their biggest fan.
They are lifetime members of my All-Star team.*

*This is also for my pal, Ron Douglas, who I first met
on a baseball field and who is a member of the
Nebraska Baseball Hall of Fame.*

*Finally, this is in memory of my dad, Jack Graves, who took
me to my first game in Yankee Stadium and bought seats
behind the dugout so I'd be close to the Mick. Dad taught me
baseball, and he showed me how to play the game.*

*As Walt Whitman reminds us,
"base-ball is our game: the American game."*

"…our joys are only the tender shadows

which our sorrows cast."

Henry Ward Beecher

1

You got moxie, kid.

Monday, April 18, 1938

We spent that last afternoon, that day before the plane spun into the tarmac, in Tom's Inn, sipping cool ones on barstools and reminiscing about the days when we played the game. It was the third Monday in April, the day after Easter Sunday, and the day the dark season would lift. Baseball would return that day to a nation of fans desperate to stow winter in the trunk and unpack warm summer days. The radio behind the bar crackled, and we strained to listen. The broadcast came in from Boston, half a continent away. Tom wiped the bar and topped off our glasses.

"Didn't you boys meet each other on a ball field?" Tom said.

We straddled our stools and grinned at each other, my pal Cocky and I, and recalled that long ago summer.

"The first words I said to him were a lie, and he knew it," I said.

"He told me he could play baseball," Cocky said. "He said he'd played the game lots of times. You were what, seven, eight years old? He didn't have a glove, and he didn't have a clue. He couldn't even find right field. All the kid had was moxie."

"Not much has changed," Tom said.

Tom stood behind the bar and readied the stick. In Boston, Jim Bagby straddled the mound in Fenway Park and rubbed a baseball between calloused palms. A light drizzle fell over ten thousand opening-day fans.

"The other guys told Cocky to send the squirt home," I said. "Cocky ignored them. He did what he wanted to do and paid no attention to their taunts and gibes."

"Not much has changed," Tom said again.

"They stared at the shrimp and kicked at the dirt," Cocky said. "They told him to come back when he'd grown a little. He was a little guy, younger than the rest of us. But we needed a right-fielder, so I tossed him a worn out piece of leather and pointed in that direction. I hoped no one would hit a ball to him. I told him if a ball came that way to pick it up off the ground and throw it back. I knew he couldn't catch a ball."

We both laughed at that.

"Except he did catch a ball, eventually," Cocky said.

"I hustled out there and waited," I said, "hands on my knees, kicking dirt like the other fellas. I chattered and waited. Then it happened, that first fly ball."

"Hold on," Tom said and poured a couple of glasses of Storz beer for his customers. He wiped his hands on a bar rag when he returned.

"Okay, go ahead," he said.

"A fly ball sailed his direction. He held up his glove, his arm as stiff as a ball bat," Cocky said. "He looked awkward, but he kept his eye on the ball. The ball grazed the leather and smacked him right in the puss."

Tom laughed. Yankee shortstop Frank Crosetti stepped into the batter's box. Crosetti screwed his spikes into the dirt and glared at Bagby, poised on the mound sixty feet and six inches away.

"He didn't quit on it, though. The shrimp stayed with it. The ball popped up and came down right in his palm. The little guy caught it. He held it up and grinned like he'd just found a shiny, green bicycle under the Christmas tree."

"The ball hit me in the eye. I wore that grin and that shiner for the rest of the day," I said.

The umpire in Boston raised a crooked finger, pointed it at the pitcher, and yelled, "Play ball!" His voice rumbled over the radio waves and traveled from the east coast to a small tavern in Wichita, Kansas. Bagby twisted his body into a windup and hurled the ball. The first pitch of the season sliced the heart of the plate, and the umpire yelled, "Stee-rike!"

A cheer rang out in Tom's Inn. Tom pulled the stick, and Storz beer flowed from the tap, first one glass, then another, and another after that. Outstretched arms and hands fisted the frothy brew. Nickels and dimes would slap onto the mahogany for the later rounds, but the first beer of the season was on the house, Tom's treat. Tom placed a beer in front of Cocky and one in front of me, and the three of us hoisted our glasses.

"To the new season," I said. "The soulless months with no baseball are no more."

"Here, here," said voices, and I watched patrons raise their glasses in the mirror behind the bar. Tom passed out White Owl cigars.

"Just like the Babe smokes," he said and lit one for himself.

We'd seen the advertisements, Babe Ruth cheek-to-cheek with wife Claire, singing the praises of a White Owl cigar. Tom blew a puff of smoke through his grin, and we hoisted our glasses again, this time in a toast to the owner of the tavern bearing his name. We smoked and drank and lied and laughed, and for one gray afternoon, we shoved aside quotidian struggles and recalled golden days of youth. For a few hours I wasn't Pete Stone, private detective. I was just an overgrown kid who loved the game. I left the grit of the city streets and roamed the grassy outfields of memory. In Beantown, Crosetti went down on strikes, and the next Yankee hitter, Red Rolfe, stepped into the batter's box.

"Hard to believe it's over, huh, winter?" Tom said. "Some folks figure it's the robin's tweet that signals spring, but not me. Winter ends when baseball begins with the first pitch."

Spring made a late appearance in Wichita that year. Earlier that month, the skies dumped a half a foot of snow on the city, the heaviest April snowfall on record. By opening day it disappeared, soaked into lawns and drained into sewers. Tom drew a beer for a customer and leaned forward, elbows on the bar.

"So, who do you boys like?"

I puffed on my cigar and furrowed my brow.

"Smart money bets on the Yanks," I said.

The peanut gallery greeted that observation with a low chorus of boos.

"They're going without DiMaggio, you know," Tom said. "He's holding out for more loot, forty grand I hear. Can you believe it? Cocky, how about you?"

Cocky missed a beat before he turned toward Tom.

"What's that?" he said.

"I got a buck says Boston takes the opener," Tom said. "Who do you like?"

"Yeah, I like the Sox, too," Cocky said. "I'll throw in a buck."

"That's two bucks on the Red Sox," Tom said and turned toward me. "You still like the Yankees, Pete?"

"I'll stay with the Yanks," I said.

We tossed our bills onto the bar. Tom scooped them up and stacked them next to the till. He moved to the tap to draw a beer for a customer. The Red Sox scored in their half of the first inning, and the Yankees countered with a pair of runs in the second. Cheers and boos followed each tally depending on the bets. Cocky cheered, too, but he was a half-beat behind the crowd. His head wasn't in the game.

"Something on your mind, Cocky?"

He looked at me for a moment and shook his head. I didn't push it. He puffed on his cigar and ordered another beer.

"You still see Lucille?" he said.

"Once in a while, sure," I said. "We go to a movie, have dinner, you know. I like her, and she says she's crazy about me. She's just not crazy about my profession."

"That's all, an occasional movie and dinner?" he said.

"No, sometimes we go out for drinks, listen to music, kick up our heels."

He waited.

"Sometimes we wake up together. We have breakfast."

"That's better," he said and gazed into his glass of beer.

"Why do you ask? What does my love life have to do with what's on your mind?" I said. "Something's bothering you. You want to talk?"

He lifted his glass and swallowed.

"No, not now. Make it Saturday night," he said. "Come out to my place on Saturday. Bring Lucille. Sundown would like that. We'll break bread. Then we'll sit on the porch and tip a jug."

Cocky lived on a farm outside of town. He worked as an aircraft mechanic in Wichita, but he and his family also worked forty acres northwest of the city.

"We can talk now," I said. "There's a table along the wall."

"No, it'll keep. Saturday night."

I didn't want to push.

"Saturday then," I said. "We'll be there."

We drank our beer and smoked our cigars and listened to the game. We shelled peanuts and popped them down the hatch and tossed the shells onto the bar. The Red Sox tied the score in the bottom of the second, but the Yankees came back with a pair in the third and led four to two. Mabel, Tom's wife, tottered out of the kitchen in the back. She carried a tray of hot dogs. Another cheer rang out in the bar. Mabel shuffled slowly and smiled at the boys. The stroke she'd suffered the previous year slowed her down, but it didn't take her from us, and we were grateful. We cheered because we hadn't lost her.

In the sixth inning Red Sox bats came alive. Bobby Doerr doubled home a pair of runners. The Sox got to Yankee pitcher Red Ruffing for six runs. Manager Joe McCarthy stewed in the dugout, paced back and forth, and rested a foot on the top step. When he'd had enough, he strode to the mound and signaled for a relief pitcher, but by then it was too late. The damage was done.

The Red Sox took the opener eight to four over the Yankees. I was out a couple of bucks, but, hey, that was baseball. We clinked our glasses and drank another beer. No one at Tom's Inn in Wichita, Kansas, stewed over an east coast baseball rivalry. The important thing was the game itself. Win or lose, baseball was back. The game signaled hope, and hope was in short supply those days. I was to learn that hope was a fickle temptress. That year she got her signals crossed. Hope flashed a light, then flickered, and finally sputtered and faded into darkness. The light went out the following day with a telephone call. A somber voice delivered the news that hit me on the chin like a high and tight fastball. It knocked me into the dirt, but I refused to stay down. I refused to yield. Instead, I got up and stood tall. When I got the news of the crash, those words Cocky spoke dozens of summers ago came back to me. Those words haunted me, and they sustained me. It was his ghost that whispered in my ear. It was his ghost that said, "You got moxie, kid. You got moxie."

2

I have bad news.

Tuesday, April 19th

The day started like any other, me in my office, feet atop my desk, a cup of Joe in one hand, and *The Wichita Eagle* in the other. Helen Hayes would appear at the Forum in *Victoria Regina* on Saturday night. It looked to be a sellout, but not for me. Saturday night I'd be with Lucille at Cocky's place. An advertisement for a movie at the Miller Theater caught my eye. *Test Pilot* starred Clark Gable and Myrna Loy. At thirty-cents a ducat, an evening at the Miller wouldn't leave much of a hole in my wallet. Maybe I'd take Lucille the following week.

I turned to the sports page. The city planned to expand the number of seats at Lawrence Stadium. The ballpark was only four years old, but it needed more room to accommodate the city's enthusiastic fans. They would add six hundred box seats at ten bucks a pop, a total of six grand. That seemed like quite an investment, but it figured to pay off. The Seth Thomas Banjo clock on the wall told me it was nine forty-five. That's when the telephone rang.

Agnes answered it at her desk outside my door then stuck her head into my office.

"It's for you."

I lowered my feet to the floor and lifted the receiver on my desk.

"Pete Stone speaking."

"Pete, Gordon Veatch here. I have bad news, so if you aren't sitting down, do it now."

Gordon Veatch was the chief engineer at Stearman Aircraft. I'd met Veatch on a case some time before, and we'd stayed in touch. Stearman made airplanes used to train military pilots. It was also the company that employed Cocky as a mechanic.

"Go ahead, Gordon."

"Your friend, Archibald Wright, died this morning. He was killed in an airplane crash. He and the pilot both perished."

Veatch said more, but the rest was just noise. The words he spoke didn't register. I tried to wrap my mind around his initial words. Cocky was dead. My pal, alive and vital one moment, was gone. We'd been together. We'd bent an elbow, straddled barstools, and grinned over the good old days. That was the day before. The next day, he was dead.

"Are you still with me, Pete?" Veatch said.

"Yeah. Yeah, I'm here. All I got was Cocky is dead. How did this happen? What can you tell me?"

"He went up this morning with one of our pilots, a routine test flight. The plane crashed shortly after takeoff. That's all I have now. It happened less than an hour ago. Pete, I'm sorry to hit you with this, but we're all shaken by it. Listen to me. The accident will be investigated, by the feds and by our people, but we haven't had time to learn much yet. It's terrible, but that's all we know now."

We paused for a moment before he continued.

"I know Wright was your friend. I'd rather lose a limb than bring you this sad news, but there's still lots to be done. That's why I'm calling you right away. We haven't contacted Wright's wife yet. She doesn't know. Now, we'll call her, but I called you first. I wondered if you'd be willing to break it to her. It's a rotten favor to ask, I know that, but she might handle it better coming from someone she knows."

Veatch was right. It was a rotten thing to ask, but it was also the right thing to do, and I said as much to Veatch.

"Yes, I'll do it," I said. "I'd rather she hear it from me. I don't want to call her. I'll drive out and talk to her. I don't want her to get this over the telephone. Someone should be with her when she takes the punch. You'll call me the minute you have more details."

"Yes, I will, and thanks, Pete," he said. "I owe you. We'll talk again soon."

The light went out and the day went dark with that telephone call. I cradled the telephone, and Agnes appeared in the doorway. She held a handkerchief and twisted it.

"Tell me I didn't hear that," she said. "I wasn't trying to listen, but I couldn't help it. I heard Cocky's name. I heard the word dead. Please tell me I didn't hear that, Pete."

I came around the desk and hugged Agnes close and felt her quiver in my arms. I held her while I told her the news and waited while she sobbed into her handkerchief. When she gained composure, I held her at arm's length.

"I have to leave," I said. "I have to tell Sundown."

Agnes nodded.

"You gather yourself," I said. "Close the office. Take the day off. Hang a sign and lock the door."

She nodded and said, "I'll be fine. You go. Give Sundown my love."

I took my hat and coat off the rack, closed the door, and left.

Sundown took the news like a fighter. She was tough, but even the toughest pug in the ring is staggered by a roundhouse to the jaw. Sundown listened, her eyes focused on a faraway place, and slumped into a straight-backed chair. She leaned forward, elbows on the checkered oilcloth that covered the kitchen table, and placed her hands over her ears, trying not to hear what she'd already heard. She shook her head from side to side and muttered "No" again and again.

I knew it would be tough, and I knew I needed help to deliver the news. I picked up Lucille at her place before I left Wichita, and I was glad I did. She shed her own tears, but by the time we reached the farm, she'd recovered like a trouper. Lucille sat beside Sundown and held her hand while I gave her the news. She ran her hand across Sundown's back and hugged her shoulders. Debbie Lynn, their daughter, sat in another straight-backed chair and wept. She held her baby and whispered, "Oh, Cindy, oh, Cindy," over and over.

I drew two glasses of water at the sink and handed one to Sundown and the other to Debbie Lynn. Lucille took baby Cindy. Sundown wiped a thin dishtowel across her eyes.

I moved to the stove to put a flame under the teakettle. Lucille joined me. She held the baby in one arm and scooped fresh coffee grounds into the coffeepot.

"Sit down," she said. "I'll take care of this."

I sat down at the table.

"Agnes sends her love," I said.

Sundown nodded and smiled. The coffee aroma stirred us, and the brew fortified us. We sipped without speaking for several minutes. When the baby fussed, Debbie Lynn took her into the next room. I smoked a cigarette and tried not to notice the condition of the kitchen. A cockroach scurried along a baseboard and disappeared behind a curled edge of wallpaper. A bucket next to the sink sat beneath a water stain on the ceiling. When we drove up earlier, I saw that the house begged for a coat of paint. Sundown read my thoughts.

"Cocky promised to fix the roof," she said. "The place just got away from us these past months. Cocky was putting in longer hours at work and not as many hours at home."

"I didn't know that. Why the long hours? What's going on at the company?" I said.

Sundown shrugged.

"He didn't talk about it, but I figured the Boeing takeover must have had something to do with it."

Cocky had been with Stearman Aircraft less than a year. He wouldn't have been there at all if not for me. I'd met Gordon Veatch the year before, on a case involving the death of one of his engineers. The engineer, Sidney Hamilton, also happened to be married to Lucille at the time. It was Lucille who came to me for help in solving the case.

Some months later, Veatch mentioned to me that Stearman was growing and would someday become a division of Boeing Corporation. They were looking for qualified personnel to bring onboard. Cocky worked for Cessna then as a certified aircraft mechanic, but Stearman made him an attractive offer, and he moved to their facility on South Oliver. Both Cocky and Sundown expected a bright future at Stearman, but that dream died when the plane went down.

"I saw Cocky yesterday," I said. "He seemed preoccupied about something, but he didn't want to talk about it. He invited us to dinner Saturday night. He said we'd talk then."

Sundown smiled at Lucille. She reached over and squeezed her hand.

"Yes, he told me that," she said. "I was tickled. I so looked forward to it."

"Maybe something at work weighed on his mind," I said. "Maybe that's what he wanted to discuss. You're right. It probably had something to do with the merger with Boeing. Deals like that tend to bring changes, some good, some not so good."

We visited a while longer. We smoked cigarettes and drank coffee. Lucille made sandwiches. Afternoon shadows grew long. Sundown glanced at the clock.

"The day's gone," she said. "You two should be getting back."

"We're fine," Lucille said.

"Should we call a neighbor to sit with you?" I said.

Sundown took a deep breath and let it out slowly.

"Not tonight. Tonight I'd like to be alone with my thoughts. Debbie Lynn and the baby are here. We'll be fine. Tomorrow I'll call neighbors, make arrangements and such, but tonight I'd just like to sit quietly with Cocky in my mind. Bless you both for coming to see us. That means so much."

We hugged and said our goodbyes and headed back to Wichita in the roadster. We drove for several minutes thinking our own thoughts before Lucille spoke.

"Those poor women," she said. "How will they ever make it?"

"It'll be tough, but they're tough, too. Sundown has traveled a bumpy road. They'll figure a way. You were terrific," I said.

"The place needs work," she said, "I don't remember it looking so run down. That wasn't like Cocky. Cocky took pride in his home. And Debbie Lynn's dress looked threadbare. She could use some clothes. I'll check my closet. I bet I have something she could wear."

We drove another mile or so.

"Tell me about Sundown," she said. "How did she and Cocky come to be? I know Debbie's mother died, but I never heard how Sundown and Cocky met."

I smiled and said, "They never talked about it much. I never knew myself until Cocky gave me the story one night. They didn't meet at a church social, that's for sure. Cocky and I had had a few drinks, more than a few, and he unloaded. Told me everything."

I thought back to the time when Cocky's wife died. Debbie Lynn had barely come into the world, and the grim reaper took her mother. They said the flu epidemic began in Kansas, the Sunflower state. That's what the experts said, anyway. They traced the beginnings to a young Army soldier who left his home in Haskell County for training at Camp Funston near Fort Riley. The soldier introduced the bug to fellow soldiers who spread it to thousands more. The virus trekked around the globe and brought sickness and death to millions worldwide. One of those dead was Cocky's wife. Lucille already knew that.

"Debbie Lynn is named for the mother who brought her into the world, the mother she never knew," I said. "Her mother died after giving birth to her. Cocky's wife caught the flu while she was in the hospital. Sundown is Debbie Lynn's mother now, the only mother she's ever known. Sundown's given name is Cynthia Downs, but Cocky gave her the new moniker. He christened her Sundown, and that's what everybody calls her.

"After his wife died, Cocky found himself alone with a newborn girl to raise. He was at a loss much of the time, but he did what he had to do. He worked hard, and he raised the girl, and he never quit, and he never complained. He did it. He cared for his daughter. He fed her and clothed her, made sure she got to school and learned her lessons. He did what needed to be done. He gave the girl a start in life, but he was a man, and a man has limitations. In her twelfth summer, Debbie Lynn became a woman. Cocky had neglected that lesson, the changes that take place in a girl's life. He hadn't given it thought, and they hadn't discussed it. His daughter wasn't ignorant. She had classmates at school, and she knew the facts of life, but she didn't have a close female friend to talk to. She was frightened and unsure, and she withdrew from Cocky. She needed a woman to confide in.

"Cynthia Downs turned out to be that woman, one of the few women Cocky knew. Cynthia lived in a two-story house on the edge of town along with six or eight other women. In the evenings, gentlemen would call at the house and visit. Downstairs, the women served whiskey and cigars to the callers. Someone played a piano. There was music and laughter. Later, men and women would pair off and move upstairs. Sometimes Cocky visited that house, and when he did, he called on Cynthia.

"That summer he called on Cynthia and told her about his daughter. He wondered if she would talk to the girl. Cynthia slipped into her shawl and reached for her handbag before Cocky finished stammering. She said she'd be pleased to help, so Cocky brought her to the farm. The women warmed to each other right away. Shortly after they met, they put their heads together and turned their backs on Cocky. He got the message and left the house to do his chores. When he returned, the women were chattering like old friends. The three of them sat down to a fine meal together.

"That evening after dinner, Cocky and Cynthia rocked in chairs on the porch and watched the sun dip below the horizon. Cocky said it was a sign. Cocky said that sunset not only ended the day, it signaled a change in their lives. Neither one mentioned the house on the edge of town again. They sat together and rocked and held hands and shared an unspoken understanding. The sun disappeared, and Cocky whispered, "Sundown." He whispered that in her ear, and he called her by that name from that moment on.

"She slept the first night on a spare bed. She slept the second night in Cocky's bed. They soon visited a justice of the peace and made it official, and Debbie Lynn began calling her Ma. That's Sundown's story as Cocky gave it to me. I never told anyone else that story. I doubt many people know it."

"It's a lovely story," Lucille said. "It'll stay with me."

3

Skinned knees and slim prospects.

Saturday, April 23rd

We arrived at the church just as Agnes and her husband, Percival Gillman, pulled up. The four of us lingered in the parking lot for a moment as other mourners moved inside. Agnes and Lucille shared a hug and chatted. Percy shook my hand.

"I'm sorry about your friend," he said and leaned in close, "and thanks for your help on that other matter. Crackerjack detective work."

That other matter Gillman referred to was a case of embezzlement at Fourth National Bank where he worked as head cashier. Nearly a thousand dollars had gone missing from a teller's drawer. The teller swore her innocence. Gillman came to see me, fedora in hand, and asked me to take care of the matter on the QT, quickly and quietly. It was an internal bank matter, and he didn't want news of the impropriety to find its way into the local papers.

I questioned the suspects one by one. The teller, a loyal employee for nearly thirty years, was innocent as were her neighboring tellers. The thief turned out to be a young intern, a college student who worked part time at the bank. He'd seen the money in the drawer and snatched it on impulse before considering the consequences. When I asked him if he'd stolen the money, he acted like he couldn't wait to confess. The guilt was killing him. Yes, he had stolen the money, and he wanted to return it. I asked the question, and he talked. No doubt about it. It was crackerjack detective work.

We went inside and sat in a pew near the rear of the church. In the crowd, I wanted to be alone with my thoughts with Lucille by my side. Sundown sat in front with Debbie Lynn beside her holding little Cindy. Cocky was not a regular church goer, and the preacher hadn't known him well. He dished out platitudes and bromides to soothe the bereaved. My thoughts drifted to bygone days spent together on the ball field. We had skinned knees, slim prospects, and more grit than talent, but death lay too far in the future to warrant our attention.

The preacher spoke his name, Archibald Wright, and I smiled. Not many folks who knew him used his given name. The man in black stood above the closed coffin and droned the Twenty-third Psalm, his voice a monotone, his gaze focused on nothing. He directed a few words to the surviving family, intoned a lengthy prayer, and lowered himself to a bench. He sat rigid above the altar, a granite statue.

The congregation delivered an uneven rendition of "Rock of Ages." Letters on the hymnal spelled out, New Hope Baptist Church. Cracks crept up the walls and meandered across the ceiling. A faded carpet ran the length of the aisle that separated rows of pews worn smooth by generations of backsides. Most of the mourners were farm families dressed in their Sunday best. A few rows up, I recognized Gordon Veatch sitting with several men who must have worked with Cocky.

Across the aisle from Veatch sat a pair of men in matching dark suits, crisp white shirts, and black ties. A blind man could see they were cops. Each sported a fresh haircut, high and tight. One was beefy and blond, big but solid. His sidekick was short and wiry with a dark complexion and brown hair.

The funeral drew to a close. The church was full, but the crowd would move on, anxious to get back to their lives. I recalled Cocky's harsh reminder about baseball and its fickle fans. "They love you when you win, they hate you when you lose, and they forget you when you're gone." *Not me, Cocky*, I thought. *I won't forget you.*

The church cleared. Friends offered condolences to the family. We went outside, and when Veatch exited we made eye contact. He waited beside his sedan and wore a grim expression.

"Come to my office Monday morning," he said.

"Has something new come up?" I said. "You can tell me now."

"Monday morning," he said. "I have to leave now. I have another one of these to attend today."

The pilot's funeral was scheduled for that afternoon. I agreed to be in his office on Monday. Lucille and I moved toward the small crowd around the family, and we all strolled to the cemetery in the cottonwoods near the church. Following the lowering of the coffin and a final prayer, I hugged Sundown. She whispered a request to meet her at her place. I nodded and assured her we'd be there.

Lucille and I walked alongside Agnes and Percival and returned to the parking lot. We said our goodbyes, and they left for Wichita. We got in the roadster and drove to the farm, and before long, we were gathered at the table in Sundown's kitchen. Lucille had brought a package wrapped in brown paper, and Debbie Lynn eyed it and wondered. Her lips were red and chapped, so she dipped a finger in a jar of Mentholatum and applied the ointment to the sore spots. When Lucille placed the package on the table in front of Debbie Lynn, the young woman smiled her surprise and began to open it. A cheap set of bracelets dangled from her left wrist, three bands of ersatz silver and turquoise. The wannabe silver had corroded and left trails of rust along her arm. Inside the package were several dresses, one yellow and one green in summer weight cotton, and a third in navy blue wool for church or dressy occasions. She "oohed" and smiled and held the dresses in front of her while Lucille held the baby. Then she ran upstairs to try them on.

Sundown brewed coffee and poured it into cups. She kissed Lucille on the cheek and thanked her, and Debbie Lynn returned to show off her fashions. Sundown nodded her approval, then she placed the spoon on the table and sighed. When she wiped her forehead with the back of her hand, her hand shook, and her fingers trembled.

"This has been a difficult week," I said. "You need to sit and rest, Sundown."

She turned and looked out the window and shook her head.

"I won't give up," she said in a quiet voice. "I won't let anyone harm my babies. No one is going to hurt my babies."

She spoke in a low voice, as if she spoke to herself and made a promise to herself, a vow she meant to keep. I looked at Lucille. She shrugged.

"What are you saying?" I said. "What do you mean?"

Sundown turned from the window and faced the room. She looked at me and then at Lucille and shook her head.

"It's going to be a struggle, what with a baby and all," she said. She put a hand on my shoulder. "Got to slop the hogs. Walk with me?"

"Go ahead," Lucille said. "I'll stay with the baby."

Sundown and I went out through the mudroom. A shotgun rested on hooks above the doorway. Boots crusted with hardened gray mud lay strewn across the floor. A worn leather baseball glove hung on a hook amid hats and jackets. Work gloves, stiff with sweat, fingers curled, lay atop a stepstool. The contents of the room formed a simple shrine to a simple man, a man who had known a hard life but embraced his work and the play that came with it. I gripped the wooden handle on the slop bucket and followed Sundown out the door. We walked down a sandy lane with cattle pens to the left and a pigsty to the right. A brown and white dog, collie mix, rose from its spot under an elm tree and fell in beside us. Sundown scratched the dog behind the ears and cooed her name, Sissy. Chickens and turkeys roamed over the lane and the pens and pecked at the ground.

"Cocky told me he was going to be a grandpa," I said. "He didn't say much else, and I didn't push."

Sundown looked down and shook her head.

"He probably didn't have much else to tell you, I suppose. Carnival came through last year, nothing more than a troupe of roving ragamuffins. A young schmoozer ran the carousel, glib and handsome. He knew what to say and just how to say it. He whispered words into Debbie Lynn's ear, and the snake's hiss charmed her. Little gal never had a fella pay her any attention as far as I know. Well, he gave her his attention, all right, along with a lesson in carnival knowledge, if you know what I mean. She succumbed. Before long, the carnival pulled up stakes, and that fella and his charm disappeared into the dust. Debbie Lynn was left with nothing to remember him by but those cheap bracelets on her arm and the beginnings of a baby."

I poured slop into the trough, and Sundown scooped in pig feed. We stood elbow-to-elbow, each with a foot on a fence rung. The hogs snorted and squealed and fought for position. A little further down the lane, the barn stood in shadows. A ramp ran from the ground to the hayloft, and a turkey stood on the ramp. I gave Sundown a puzzled look, and she explained.

"That was Cocky's idea," she said, "to control grasshoppers. He bought a couple hundred baby turkeys a couple of years back. Our henhouse wouldn't hold them, so he raised them in the loft. They learned to use the ramp and went up at night to roost. We raised them to eat grasshoppers, those miserable little critters. Grasshoppers ate everything in their path. The turkeys feasted on them, and that helped save our crops. We didn't have to buy feed for the birds at all."

She paused and looked down at the dog and petted it again.

"This has been an awful week, Sundown," I said. "You don't

deserve what's happened, but there's something else, isn't there? Something besides Cocky's death is bothering you. Talk to me."

Sundown nodded and looked down at the ground.

"Yes, you're right. I'm scared, Pete. I'm plumb scared. Not for me, mind you, but I'm frightened for my little girls. Losing Cocky is bad enough, but if anything happened to those girls, I don't believe I could bear it."

"What is it? What happened?" I said. "What's frightened you?"

She raised her head and gazed at the hogs.

"A man came by," she said, "ugly man. Thick eyebrows, scar down the side of his nose, coarse hair on the backs of his hands, hairy fingers, too. He wore a rumpled suit and needed a shave and a bath. He drove a dusty Ford with Michigan plates. I watched him come down the drive from the kitchen window. When he stopped, he didn't get out of his car right away. He just sat behind the wheel and looked around like he was casing the place. He gave me the heebie-jeebies. When he finally did get out of his car, he had a scowl on his face. He looked dangerous, and I was scared. I didn't want that man inside the house, so I met him outside on the walk before he could get to the door.

"He didn't say hi, hello, or any other pleasantry. He just began ranting. He talked about Cocky. He claimed that Cocky had something that belonged to him, and he intended to get it back. I told him I didn't know what he was talking about, which is the God's honest truth, and if he knew what was good for him he'd get off my property while he still could. He said he wasn't leaving until he got what he came for. He reached under his coat and pulled out a gun and pointed it at me. I've been around some rough men in my time, but no one ever pointed a gun at me before. He yelled at me, 'Where is it?'

"I didn't know what he meant, and I didn't care. I was scared, Pete. All I could think about was Debbie Lynn and that little baby. The man had a gun. What that man didn't know was that I had a gun, too, a shotgun hidden under my apron. His eyes went wide when I pulled it out. He froze, and that was all I needed. I gave him both barrels."

Neither one of us spoke for a moment. We listened to the hogs grunt and snort. A meadowlark called in the distance. A forlorn calf bawled in the pen across the lane. Sundown rested her elbows atop the fence and gazed into the sty.

"And Debbie Lynn was inside the house when his happened?" I said.

"She was with the baby, upstairs. She heard the shots. She asked about them."

"What did you tell her?"

"I told her the truth. I told her I shot and killed a varmint."

"You're something," I said. "Cocky always said you were long on courage. You were frightened, but you held up. You did what you had to do."

She nodded.

"I suppose I did," she said.

"You said the man was unshaven and drove a car with Michigan tags. He came a long way. Someone must have sent him here. If that's the case, someone else may show up."

Sundown nodded and said, "I thought of that. That's what scares me. What if I don't get the drop on the next one? What then? And what did this guy want, anyway? What did Cocky have that he wanted?"

"I don't know," I said, "but I intend to find out."

"I figured you say that," she said. "Part of me was hoping you wouldn't get involved, but I knew better."

She hesitated before she reached into a pocket of her dress.

"Cocky left this on top of the dresser in our bedroom."

She handed me an unsealed envelope. STONE was printed in pencil across the front. Inside I found a small brass key. Nothing else. No note, just the key.

"What do you make of this?" I said. "Do you know what this key opens?"

"No idea," she said.

"Why no note?"

"Maybe he felt he didn't need one. Maybe he intended to tell you about it over dinner," she said.

"That could be," I said. "Just a key, and not much of a key at that. Did he have a lockbox, a diary, anything this might belong to?"

"Cocky? A diary? Not hardly," she said. "He never wrote in a diary, and that man never locked a thing, house included."

I puzzled over the key. I didn't understand it, but I didn't want to lose it, either. I slipped it onto my keychain and tucked the empty envelope into my coat pocket.

"I have another question," I said.

"Of course you do. You want to know what I did with the body."

I nodded. She gazed into the sty and took a deep breath before she spoke.

"Them hogs gotta eat, too," was all she said.

We drove away from the farm that afternoon. I noticed a weathered outbuilding. A green bike leaned against it. The building's door was ajar, and inside I glimpsed the dusty fender of a black Ford. Cocky's family was in for a struggle, but they'd make it. Sundown remained tough and controlled her fear. She was like a batter in the late innings facing down a pitcher with the game on the line. She'd dig in her spikes and keep swinging.

4

You've fallen down
the wrong hole, Alice.

Saturday, April 23rd

We drove over county roads to the south and east toward Wichita. The sun dropped, and the shadows lengthened. Lucille dozed in the passenger seat. A day spent sitting and mourning had exhausted us both. I mulled over my conversation with Sundown and wondered who the stranger was and why he had appeared at the farm. I wondered what was so valuable to him that he had threatened Sundown with a gun. What did Cocky have that he wanted? Cocky left a key in an envelope, but he died before he told me what the key unlocked. And then there was Gordon Veatch. What did he have to tell me? I wouldn't know that until Monday.

I approached an intersection. A rooster-tail of dust appeared in my mirror. It looked to be a half-mile or so back. When we left the farm, I noticed a sedan in my wake, but the light had faded and was too dim to tell if the sedan was the source of the dust cloud. Most anyone from the country could be driving to Wichita for a Saturday night on the town. It grew darker, and I turned on my headlights

Sundown said Cocky had worked longer hours lately, and he'd spent less time at home. Maybe Veatch could explain why that was. Something had been on his mind that last day we were together, but he wouldn't tell me until he was ready. He did things his own way, in his own time.

Cocky's hero and namesake was Eddie Collins, second baseman for the Chicago White Sox. Collins was a star with such talent and self-confidence that his teammates christened him, Cocky. My pal adopted the position and the moniker for himself, and he was suited to both. He strutted when he won, but he didn't gloat, and he never badgered an opponent. He respected the game, he respected himself, and he respected his opponent. Win or lose, he carried himself with dignity and assurance.

The headlights behind me followed my roadster into the city. West Street marked the edge of town. I turned south and dropped to Second Street. The headlights stayed back several car lengths but matched my turns. We moved into a residential area, and at Clarence I turned right. The sedan continued traveling east on Second. I glimpsed a pair of silhouettes in the car.

I pulled up at Lucille's place, and she roused awake.

"Sorry," she said. "I haven't been very good company."

"You were terrific," I said. "I'd have been lost at sea without you to help with Sundown and Debbie Lynn."

At the door I kissed her goodnight. Our kiss grew longer, and I squeezed her tighter. Her eyes widened.

"Pete, I'm exhausted. I have to sleep."

"I'll put you to bed," I said.

"Sure you will. You're incorrigible. Go home and go to bed."

She went inside and blew a kiss at me with a smile before she disappeared behind the closed door. I got back into the roadster. I was famished and thirsty and wanted refreshment, but I'd neglected the office for the past few days, and Agnes had taken time off, too. I needed to check my mail and messages. I drove south another block to Douglas and turned east and crossed over the bridge spanning the Arkansas River. Traffic was light, but a number of cars were parked on the street near Broadway south of the Miller and Orpheum Theaters, Saturday night movie-goers I figured.

I pulled over to the curb past the intersection of Douglas and Emporia near the entrance to the Lawrence Block building. Robert Lawrence had been a city founder, and Charles Lawrence was a former mayor, and the Lawrence named often appeared around the city. My office was on the third floor of the building. A dark sedan rolled by, and the short hairs on my neck stood on end. I reached under the dash and freed the Smith and Wesson .38 from its rack and slipped it into my pocket.

The building was dark and unoccupied, but ambient light from the street allowed me to navigate the lobby and climb the shadowed stairs. I unlocked the door to the outer office, switched on a light, and stooped to pick up the mail on the floor beneath the slot. Nothing important caught my eye, so I dropped the pile on Agnes's desk. The only telephone message was from my mechanic reminding me that my roadster was due for a tune-up. The mechanic was one of the few men in town who had worked for the Jones Motor Car Company before it closed its doors. I slipped the message in my pocket.

My desk in the inner office was tidier than I'd left it. Agnes had emptied the brass ashtray and wiped it clean. She also tossed the remnants of a tuna fish sandwich I'd eaten for lunch a day earlier. Everything looked in order, and I turned to leave when I heard the outer door open. I ducked behind my door and took my gun out of my pocket. When the intruders entered my office, I stepped from behind the door and leveled my gun at them.

"Hold it right there and put your hands where I can see them," I said.

The pair turned their faces toward me and eyeballed my hardware. Neither showed alarm. They reacted as if staring down the barrel of a gun was all in a day's work. The large man and his wiry companion still wore their matching black suits.

"No reason to point a gun," the large man said. "Be careful with that heater. This isn't what it looks like."

"What does it look like?" I said. "It looks to me like a couple of intruders just broke into my office looking to get the jump on me, that's what it looks like."

"We're not crooks, and you know it," he said. "Either you made us for cops this morning at the church or you're the lousiest gumshoe in this backwater hamlet."

"You creep around like crooks," I said. "Give. What is this?"

"First, lose that heater," he said. "Let me reach for my ID."

I lowered the gun but kept it in my hand, and the big guy reached into his pocket.

"Nice and easy," I said. "Real slow."

He pulled out a wallet and flashed a gold shield.

"Hand it over."

He did, and I studied it. It identified the man as Leonard Young, agent of the FBI. I handed it back to him.

"How about junior here? Does the little guy own similar ID?" I said.

The little guy looked like he didn't appreciate the reference to his size.

"Show him your badge, George," the blond said to his partner.

I did a double take.

"George? Leonard?" I said. "That's rich."

I looked from one to the other and laughed into my fist. A recent novel, *Of Mice and Men,* featured a hapless pair of characters called George and Lennie.

"What's so funny?" the little guy said. He clinched his fists and stuck out his jaw.

"Not a thing," I said and shook my head.

"Show him your badge," Young said again.

"Forget it. I could read it all right, but Roscoe here can't read," I said and nodded at my gun. "Roscoe gets nervous, and when Roscoe gets nervous he speaks. Loud."

"Take it easy and put that gun away," Agent Young said.

I looked from one man to the other and pocketed my pistol.

"My partner is George Townsend. We're both with the FBI," Young said.

"No kidding. That would explain your dashing wardrobes," I said. "That still doesn't explain what you're doing here. I suppose it was you two who followed me into town this evening. What're you after anyway? I don't suppose you've got a warrant?"

Young moved toward his coat pocket again and pulled out a folded paper. He handed it to me.

"You didn't get a warrant this evening," I said. "You must've had it earlier."

I looked it over. It was issued the day before.

"Okay, what's this about?" I said. "What are you looking for, and what makes you think I have it?"

"This involves your deceased friend. We have reason to believe he had something that didn't belong to him, something he may have hidden, or something he may have given to a friend. If you have it, you know what it is. If you don't have it, there's no reason to discuss it with you."

"Let's ignore for a moment the fact that Cocky Wright was an upstanding and honest citizen. If you fellows think my pal was on the wrong side of the law, then you're even bigger chumps than I take you for. That aside, why are you here now? Why are you following me?"

"You spent a lot of time at the farm this afternoon," he said. "Maybe the widow told you something. Maybe she gave you something. Maybe you could save us a lot of time and trouble and hand it over."

"Yeah, and maybe the sea is boiling hot, and maybe pigs have wings. You've fallen down the wrong hole, Alice, you and the mad hatter here. It's late, and I'm tired, too tired to dance the waltz with the likes of you two."

"I don't think he likes us," little George said.

I shrugged and said, "I wouldn't fret over that, Georgie, boy.

There's lots of guys I don't like. Guys who sneak into my office without knocking land at the top of the list."

"Okay, Stone," Young said, "suppose you empty your pockets?"

"Suppose you take a hike."

"If we take a hike, you're taking it with us."

I shrugged and emptied the contents of my pockets onto the desk, my gun, my wallet, my keychain, a handful of change, a pocketknife, an opened pack of Chesterfield cigarettes, a book of matches, a pencil, my notebook, the message from my mechanic, and the empty envelope with my name penciled across the front of it. Young thumbed through my notebook. Townsend looked inside my wallet and tossed it back onto the desk. Young picked up the message, read it, and dropped it. He picked up the envelope and looked inside.

"This envelope is empty," he said. "What was in here?"

I said, "My friend left that for me. Inside was a recipe."

Young raised an eyebrow.

"Yeah, a recipe for peach cobbler," I said. "Cocky baked a terrific peach cobbler, best I've ever tasted. He promised to leave me the recipe in his will."

Little George looked like he was ready to explode. A vein bulged on his forehead.

"Don't crack wise," he said.

"What? You don't like peach cobbler, George? You should try it sometime. It might sweeten your disposition."

"Take it easy, Stone," Young said. "So, where's the recipe?"

"I ate it," I said.

"Let me bust him," George said. "Just once, let me bust him one across the mouth."

I laughed and said, "You better leave the heavy work to the big guy, small stuff. I doubt you'd leave a mark."

That really steamed his oysters. His eyes held fury.

"You know, you guys have it backwards," I said. "In the book, George was the smart one."

Little George looked baffled.

"What's this guy talking about? What book?"

"Forget it," Young said. "I don't know what was in this envelope, but it couldn't have held what we're looking for. It's not big enough to hold what we want."

"Not that it's any of your business," I said, "but the envelope was empty when I got it. If my friend meant to put anything in it, he died before he got around to it."

Leonard tossed the envelope onto the desk.

"I suppose we could search your office," he said, "but you just got here. How about it? Are you hiding anything?"

"Yeah. In the bottom drawer of my desk I stashed a bottle of rye. Pull it out and crack the seal. We'll drink to the memory of the pal I lost."

Little George looked like he wanted to rip my throat out. Leonard Young remained cool and surrendered the trace of a smile. He shook his head and put on his hat.

"I guess we'll crack the seal on that bottle of rye another time," he said. He ushered George out of the office and closed the door behind them.

5
The elevators failed.

Monday, April 25th

Cocky once hoped to play professional ball, but what young kid with a glove and a bat didn't? We harbored dreams of digging our spikes into the batter's box and hearing the roar of the fans. The urchins we played with would have sold their souls to stare down a big league pitcher like Lefty Grove or Mel Harder. Cocky, though, had the talent, but he never caught the eye of a scout, not on the remote patches of dirt we roamed.

Cocky married a sweet gal, fathered a daughter, and anticipated a quiet life, but fate dealt him a rotten hand. He never played in Yankee Stadium, and he lost his wife too soon. She died with the flu, and she never got to see her daughter grow up. When she died, a piece of Cocky died, too. The fire in his eyes didn't go out, but the glow dimmed. Little Debbie Lynn kept the flame alive. She gave him purpose and reason to carry on, to do what had to be done. He farmed and provided for his daughter, and he provided for Sundown, too. After she became a part of the family, Cocky wanted more than a forty acre patch of ground could provide.

The Depression left men across the country without jobs, but Wichita kindled a spark in entrepreneurs that gave birth to industries and businesses that thrived. Mentholatum was created late in the previous century, and shortly after that, the Coleman Company was founded. Various food stores and restaurants sprang up, and some branched into chain locations, but it was the aviation industry that put Wichita on the map. The city became known as the "Air Capital of the World."

Cocky had tinkered with machines all his life, and he figured he had a future as an airplane mechanic. He went to work for Cessna and became a certified mechanic, and stayed with them for several years until Stearman Aircraft lured him away. When Gordon Veatch told me the company was looking for good men, I introduced him to Cocky, and Cocky was hired soon after. That morning I was on the way to meet with Gordon Veatch in his office.

I motored south on Oliver toward Stearman headquarters. I crossed Pawnee and turned in the drive near the intersection of Oliver and 31st Street South. I parked the roadster and heard the sounds of planes above. A pair of blue and yellow biplanes, Kaydet Trainers, soared in a cloudless sky. Pilots put the aircraft through their paces. Men in shirt sleeves and ties clustered on the field and made notations on their clipboards. A pilot dove and pulled up in a V fashion and then repeated the maneuver. The other pilot approached the runway, touched down, and accelerated back into the sky.

A hangar with oversized doors standing open was next to the offices. Workers in the hangar labored on similar blue and yellow biplanes. New Kaydet planes were arrayed in a row along the tarmac outside the hangar. A heavyset man in dungarees peered into the cockpit of one of the planes and made some notes on a clipboard. He glanced at the planes overhead and used a bandana to wipe off his forehead and crew cut scalp. I went into the office. A secretary I'd met before, Mrs. Richeson, sat behind a typewriter and greeted me with a smile that crossed her face in a straight line.

"Mr. Veatch is expecting you," she said.

She led me to Veatch's office, the same office I'd visited on previous occasions. Nothing had changed but the sign on the door. His name had a new title, Senior Vice President. I found him inside in his usual posture, his short, stocky frame hunched over a drafting table, sleeves rolled to the elbows, and an unlit stub of a cigar jutting from the corner of his mouth. He stood up and removed the stub with one hand and shook my hand with the other. He leaned toward his secretary and spoke.

"Tell them he's here," he said.

She nodded and left, and he turned back to me.

"Thanks for coming," he said.

He moved to a padded swivel chair behind his desk and gestured toward a straight-backed chair across from him. An open window brought a breeze and the drone of aircraft into the room. I took a seat, and he settled back and opened with questions about my business. We discussed the gumshoe biz for a moment, then he asked about Cocky's widow, how was she holding up? That sort of thing. I began to wonder why I was there, but I told him about my visit with Sundown after the funeral. I didn't mention her encounter with the gun-toting stranger. He listened and nodded when I replied. Then gave me an update on the aircraft industry and held forth on the future of Stearman vis-à-vis Boeing. That was the expression he used, vis-à-vis. Again, I wondered why I was there and where this conversation was headed. For a guy with something important to say, Veatch was traveling a roundabout route to say it, but I remained patient.

He informed me that Stearman's president, Earl Schaefer, had been promoted to first vice-president of Boeing, and the merger assured there would be no dismissal of Stearman personnel. All of its employees would remain on the job. The conversation was pleasant, enlightening, and offered not a single clue as to why I had been summoned to his office. I wasn't interested in the aircraft business. Veatch was stalling, and my patience wore thin. He read my face. He leaned forward, his brow furrowed.

"Stone, it's a pleasure to see you, but too often when our paths cross, death is involved. You and Wright were friends, of course. I know that. It's why I wanted to talk to you. His death is a terrible loss." He paused and added, "I admired him."

He held a flame to his cigar stub. I lit a cigarette and waited for the shoe to drop. Veatch's comment troubled me. Had he used the past tense because Cocky was gone or because Veatch's admiration had waned?

He said, "You said you visited with Mrs. Wright after the funeral."

"That's right, at the farm. We dredged up memories of Cocky and rehashed stories from when we were young. She and Cocky were good for each other. She's a strong woman, been kicked around some. Now, her husband is gone, a tough punch to the midsection, but she's a survivor. That's not why you asked me here, Gordon. You didn't summon me to discuss old memories and ponder a widow's future. Why am I here? What's on your mind?"

Veatch removed the cigar from his mouth and leaned back in his chair. His eyes didn't waver. Neither did mine. After a long moment, he dropped the cigar stub into an astray and let it smolder.

An intercom on the desk buzzed, and a feminine voice said, "They're here." Veatch pushed a button and said, "Show them in."

To me he said, "You're about to get your answer."

Mrs. Richeson opened the door and stepped aside. Two men entered, one blond and beefy, the other dark and wiry, each dressed in a dark suit, cleaned and pressed. I wondered if they had their suits pressed every night or if copies of the same style hung in their closets. My money was on the latter. They looked at Veatch and then at me, and I tipped my head back and laughed. Veatch threw me a look like I'd gone bananas.

"You've met these men?" he said.

"Sure, we're old pals," I said. "The tall one is Mutt, and shorty there is Jeff. I met them in the funny papers. Real cutups, the pair of them."

"Always the wise guy," little George said. "Just once, I'd like to teach you some manners. Just once."

"Easy, George," Leonard Young said. "Don't let him rile you."

Veatch shook his head.

"Well, you've met each other," he said. "That would explain the animosity. Since there's no need for introductions, let's get started."

He gestured toward a table in a corner, and we all took a seat.

"Stone was telling me that he visited the widow after the funeral," Veatch said.

"Yes, we know he was at the farm," Agent Young said. "We've been over that. He hasn't told us a thing worth hearing. Stone likes to play it cagey. He holds his cards close to the vest."

"Cagey?" I said. "You two followed me to the farm. You two dogged me back to Wichita. You strolled into my office at night without so much as a by your leave. You questioned me. You had me empty my pockets. You found nothing. Cagey? You guys wrote the book on cagey. I don't know what you're after, but whatever it is, I don't have it. It looks like Veatch is involved in your shenanigans. Why don't you clowns come clean? What's going on? Why is the FBI interested in a private eye and a dead airplane mechanic?"

The three of them exchanged glances. Young spoke.

"Are you familiar with the German American Bund?"

"The German American Bund?" I said. "What are you talking about? Where did that come from? All I know is what I read. They're a political group, homegrown radicals, a version of the Nazi party, I suppose. I'm not on their mailing list, and I've never spoken to a member. I don't think I'd care to."

"You have spoken to a member," Young said. "Maybe you didn't know it, maybe you did. You and Archibald Wright were friends. Wright belonged to the German American Bund."

"I don't believe you, and even if I did, it wouldn't matter. You bet we were friends. Cocky was my pal. So, what? Where are you headed with this?"

"We're interested in your friend's politics. What can you tell us about that?" George said.

His eyes squinted, and he jutted his jaw. It made a tempting target for my clenched fist.

"I'll tell you what I know. Cocky's politics were the same as mine, and they were the same as yours and the same as every other American who votes. He voted by secret ballot, and I do, too. We kept it to ourselves. We didn't discuss politics. Even if I did know how Cocky voted, I wouldn't discuss it with you. That would be none of your business."

I turned to Veatch and said, "Why am I here? Why are these bozos here? Does this have anything to do with Cocky's death? Tell me what you know, and tell me why I'm on the hot seat."

"Take it easy," he said. "I agree with you. Keep your politics private, that's my policy. Personally, I don't give a tinker's dam about this Bund and who belongs to it. What I do care about is Stearman Aircraft, its people, and its products. We've discovered something troubling, and that's why you're here."

"Slow down. Choose your words," Young said.

"Oh, pshaw," Veatch said. "I know this man, and we need his help. He deserves to know what I know."

"What do you know?" I said.

"The plane crashed shortly after takeoff," Veatch said. "It was a routine flight. The pilot had detected a troublesome noise he couldn't identify, nothing serious, something in the fuselage he thought. The plane flew fine, but he wanted a mechanic to check it out."

"So Cocky checked it out," I said. "What did he find?"

"He inspected it on the ground, and everything looked fine," he said. "Nothing looked out of order, but he agreed to go up with the pilot."

"Everything checked out, so they went up and crashed," I said. "That makes no sense, an experienced pilot and a working plane."

"Not so fast. Wright checked the plane, alright. That was Monday. Wright suggested they take it up then, but the pilot couldn't do it. He had an appointment downtown. Wright had also asked to leave early that day, according to his supervisor. I guess it was to meet you."

"Yeah, we were together Monday afternoon, in a tavern listening to a baseball game."

"So, the pilot and Wright agreed to go up first thing Tuesday morning."

"Right before you called me."

"That's right," he said. "Everything I've told you is information we've gathered from men in the shop."

I looked at the FBI agents in their black suits. They had questioned the men in the shop, no doubt. Their expressions revealed nothing. I didn't know why they were at Stearman, and I didn't know what they wanted from me. I had questions, but I held my tongue and let Veatch continue.

"We investigated the wreckage," he said. "We determined that the cables to the elevators malfunctioned and caused the plane to crash."

"Elevators?" I said.

"That's right. Elevators adjust the pitch of the aircraft, up or down. They allow the pilot to lift the nose on takeoff or lower the nose to land safely. The cables to those elevators were unattached, broken, severed, call it what you will. The elevators failed after takeoff."

"Everything checked out on Monday, but on Tuesday, these elevators failed," I said.

"They failed soon after takeoff. They worked on the ground. Pilots run a preflight check that includes testing the elevators. They worked during preflight."

"They worked, and then they failed?" I said. "The wreckage

must have been a mess. How can you be sure the elevators caused the crash? Maybe those cables tore loose on impact. How can you be sure it wasn't engine failure or something else?"

"It could have been something else," he said, "but witnesses saw the plane nose into the ground. An engine malfunction wouldn't cause that. A pilot can glide a plane with no engine and land it safely, certainly with a runway below him. The engine didn't fail. That plane nosed in because the pilot lost control, and a plane without elevators flies no better than a dead pigeon. We suspect the elevators failed."

"Okay, the elevators failed," I said. "Are you suggesting they'd been tampered with, compromised? Why did they fail? Was the cable worn? Was it cut? Could it have been loosened so it would work during the preflight check and fail after takeoff? If somebody planned for this to happen, why? Who would do this and why? What are the answers?"

I paused and stared hard at the FBI agents.

"Why is the FBI here?" I said. "Don't tell me these men are here to investigate failed aircraft elevators and the deaths of two Stearman employees. Something is going on. What is it? What's the connection between a plane wreck and the German American Bund, and why are my friend's remains planted six feet underground?"

Veatch looked at the two other men. The buzz of aircraft above came through the open window. Agent Young returned Veatch's look and shrugged.

"It's your show," he said.

Veatch turned back to me.

"You're asking the right questions. We have the same questions, but we don't have all the answers."

"Tell me what you do know," I said.

"You're right about one thing. These FBI agents aren't here to investigate a plane crash. They were here already, investigating another matter. You know that Stearman has become a division of

Boeing. Everything will be finalized in the next few weeks, provided nothing happens before then to queer the deal. That's where the FBI comes in. We've discovered evidence of espionage at both Stearman and Boeing."

"Espionage? What does this have to do with my friend?" I said.

"We've discovered photographs taken of technology still in development, sensitive matters intended to be secret to all but a few. That's all you need to know. When we learned this, my superiors reported it to the FBI. They have reason to believe that the material we found was to be given or sold to the German American Bund, perhaps to be funneled on to Hitler's regime in Germany. That would be tragic, especially if we were to one day find ourselves at war with Germany."

"Photographs, espionage," I said. "I'm slow, but I'm trainable. Connect the dots for me. What does this have to do with a plane crash that took my friend?"

Veatch bit the tip off of a fresh cigar and spat it into a wastebasket.

"After the accident, one of our men gathered up Wright's personal effects to be returned to his widow," he said. "This man found something disturbing in Wright's toolbox, buried beneath a tray of wrenches. This man found a half dozen photographs, photographs of parts inside one of our aircraft, six photographs that never should have been taken and that had no business being in your friend's possession. That's why you're here. You're here because we're looking for answers, and you were Wright's friend. Why did he have those photographs, and what was he going to do with them? We want answers, and maybe you have those answers. Of course, we'd love to talk to Wright himself, but unfortunately Mr. Wright is no longer talking."

6

A foul taste.

Monday, April 25th

“What a terrible thing to say about your friend. I didn't know Cocky as well as you did, but I still don't believe it. Accusing him of taking photographs and stealing plans from Stearman, espionage of all things. That's not the man I knew, and it's not the man you've talked about so many times. Something smells like rotten fish.”

Agnes sounded as steamed as I felt. She harbored the soul of a spitfire, and when she set her jaw and clenched her fists, it behooved a wise person to beware. I'd left Stearman moments before and returned to my office to consider the conversation we'd had and to make a telephone call. I had just cradled the receiver when Agnes came into my office and delivered her tirade.

“Now what?” she said. “What's next? What are you going to do about it?”

I stood up from my desk and put on my hat.

“I'm going to work. I'm going to meet with a man I know. I need a history lesson,” I said.

Agnes raised an eyebrow and puzzled over that remark. She watched as I crossed the floor and closed the door behind me.

The campus of the Municipal University of Wichita lay to the north and east of downtown. Ethan Alexander, history professor, taught classes at the university. I had called for an appointment to meet with him. Alexander had mentored my son, Dan, during his years of graduate studies, and he had also assisted me on cases in the past, including a murder case the previous year. I admired and respected his intelligence and broad knowledge.

I motored east in my roadster. A couple of blocks past the Eaton Hotel, several ragged men loitered outside Union Station. A train hissed and snorted on the tracks. A diner had opened its doors down the street, Curley's Inn, near the intersection of Douglas and Washington. A new business signaled hope, and I vowed to sample its chow. Further on, I passed by two schools, Roosevelt Intermediate School and Wichita High School next door. Youngsters at recess tossed softballs and chased each other over the lawn. At the intersection with Grove, a man carrying his belongings on his back held his hat in his hand and watched the traffic go by.

I went on toward Hillside where I turned north. At Ninth, Hillside bisected a pair of graveyards, Highland Cemetery on the left and Maple Grove Cemetery on the right. As a kid, I held my breath when I passed a cemetery, a silly superstition. That was many years and a lot of cigarettes ago, and on this day I did not hold my breath. I figured my resting spot beneath a shade tree would arrive soon enough. I'd have plenty of time to hold my breath then.

At Seventeenth I turned right and in two blocks reached Fairmount where I turned left and rolled onto the campus bound for the Liberal Arts building. The harsh realities of the city streets fell behind and out of mind, replaced by the gentle landscape of the campus. Pear and apple trees bloomed, along with redbuds and lilacs. Students strolled on walks that wound between beds of phlox and tulips and other seasonal flowers. Worries of the world existed, but those worries lay beyond the campus borders. Maybe they realized it or maybe they didn't, but students and faculty alike shared a soft berth at the university.

I parked my roadster near a tan Hudson I'd seen before. It belonged to an English professor I knew. I entered the Liberal Arts building and found Ethan Alexander in his office, Room 113, hunched over his desk and reading student papers. Final exams loomed a few weeks ahead. Alexander probably had exams to prepare and essays to grade, but when I called him that morning, he insisted I come right over. I knocked on the open door, and his booming voice greeted me.

"Pete! Come in! Come in! It's good to see you, a breath of fresh air. Fresh air is something this room could use."

The air in his office was dusty and smoky, as usual. He laughed and spun his wheelchair toward the window and heaved it upward.

"Sit down! Sit down!"

He motioned to a straight-backed chair in front of the desk that was stacked with papers. I transferred the papers to the floor and sat down. Ethan's office hadn't changed a whit since my last visit months earlier. Disordered books crammed the shelves, and papers were stacked atop all horizontal surfaces. Dust and pipe smoke wafted in the air.

The history professor, lord of his domain, beamed a smile from his wheelchair, a souvenir and parting gift for his contributions during the Great War two decades prior. It was good to see him. The cluttered office with its cloudy air rivaled a barstool at Tom's Inn or a box seat at Lawrence Stadium for coziest spot in town.

Ethan made visitors feel welcome, but I knew he was busy, and I didn't want to waste his time. I told him about Cocky's death and about the FBI visiting my office, and I told him about the meeting we'd had in Veatch's office earlier that day. Ethan listened and offered condolences on the death of my friend. He grumbled when I mentioned the German American Bund, but held his tongue and allowed me to continue.

"They're accusing my friend of being a spy," I said. "That's baloney. My friend is dead. He can't speak for himself, but I intend to speak for him. The plane crash is being treated as an accident, but maybe it wasn't an accident. Maybe the elevators on the plane were tampered with. I'm convinced the photographs in his toolbox were a plant, put there by someone else. The FBI claims Cocky belonged to the Bund. I'm going to find out and get to the bottom of this. I'm going to clear Cocky Wright's name, but I need information. Can you tell me anything about this Bund organization?"

"The German American Bund," he said and frowned as he spat out the words. "Certainly not my brand of politics, but to each his own."

"It sounds like you're familiar with the group. What can you tell me?" I said. "If there's a connection between the Bund and my friend, I intend to find it. I need some insight. What makes them tick? What are their motives, that sort of thing?"

Ethan nodded and wheeled around his desk to one of the bookshelves. He pulled a folder stuffed with paper off of the shelf. He reached into a desk drawer and retrieved a similar looking folder. As he thumbed through the papers, he delivered an off-the-cuff overview of Chancellor Adolf Hitler, a man possessed with hypnotic powers of speech whose mesmerizing assurance enthralled throngs of followers. Hitler spewed outrageous statements, many totally false, but the sheep in the flock never questioned their veracity. They baaed and swallowed and cried for more. Hitler's ideology called for the Aryan race to dominate the world. I listened to Ethan's lecture without comment.

"Forgive me," he said. "I tend to go on. I apologize. You're not a student. You're a detective, and you're trying to solve a case. You aren't preparing a dissertation."

"Thanks. We don't have time to go through the entire bible, but I could use a chapter and verse."

"Fair enough," he said.

The first folder contained photos and clippings from

newspapers and magazines. He handed me a photograph of a man with a square chin and an intense stare. He was dressed in a military uniform. Another photograph showed the same man paying his respects to Adolf Hitler. Other photos showed him delivering speeches before crowds of people, sometimes surrounded by men in uniform who appeared to be a security detail.

"That's Fritz Kuhn," he said, "leader of the German American Bund. Kuhn is a naturalized American citizen. Until recently, he worked at a Ford plant in Detroit, but the man was born in Germany, and he fought as an infantryman in the Great War."

Ethan paused and grasped the arms of his wheelchair. My thoughts went to the man who had visited Sundown at the farm. That man had arrived in a Ford with Michigan plates. He would have harmed Sundown to get what he wanted, but she derailed his plans with a shotgun blast and added his corpse to the menu for the hogs. Ethan stared at his desk for a moment before he continued.

"Even though he's a citizen of this country, Kuhn continues to support Hitler and his policies. He travels throughout the country and stirs passions in his followers. Members hold meetings all over, including here in Wichita I suspect."

He handed me more photographs. Boys at a youth camp, lads too young to know their own minds, wore short-pants uniforms and adopted the serious facial expressions of their fathers. In another photo, boys in uniform marched in a parade in front of adults who offered the Nazi salute. At a rally in New York, onlookers saluted an American flag hanging alongside a Nazi swastika.

Ethan thumbed through clippings and read aloud bits of columns and commentaries from newspapers and magazines, local and national. *The Wichita Eagle, The New York Times,* and *The Atlantic Monthly* reported on Bund activities throughout the country. Confrontations and riots often ensued at these gatherings. Editorials, pro and con, discussed the Bund and its philosophies. A common thread was a disdain for democracy and an embrace of fascism. The Aryan race was the master race, and people of mixed races, along with Jews and Negroes, were deemed inferior. Ethan finished reading. He leaned back and lit his pipe. I lit a cigarette.

"Talking about all this leaves a foul taste in my mouth," he said, and I agreed.

"What do you know about local activities?" I said. "Is the Bund active here?"

He thought for a moment.

"I don't know how active they are in Wichita," he said, "but it shouldn't be difficult to find out. Start with politics. Listen to the political candidates, some of them, anyway. This is an election year. I've noticed that a few candidates running for office express positions remarkably similar to those of the Bund. That doesn't mean they're members of the organization, you understand. Still, I find it troubling, but that's just my opinion. Others may find what they say to their liking."

I asked him to tell me more.

"There's a fellow here in Wichita, both a preacher and a publisher. His name is Alfred Warren. He's running for the senate. He advocates racial segregation and anti-Semitism, as does the Bund. Another local citizen, Raymond Tipple, publishes a weekly rag called *Spotlight*. He supports Warren and others of his ilk. I'd don't have a copy of the paper, but it's easy enough to locate a copy."

I noted what he said in my book and thanked him for his time. I rose to leave.

"Wait a second," he said. "This came to me in the mail."

He handed me a flier that announced a luncheon to be held at the Forum the following day. Candidates for political offices were scheduled to speak.

"You might want to attend that," he said, "and take this along with you. Read it later."

He handed me another paper folded into thirds. I stuck it into my pocket and thanked him again before I left. I drove back toward downtown and mulled over the information about the German American Bund that Ethan had shared with me. He was right. Even though he'd done most of the speaking, it left a bad taste in my mouth, too. I was convinced that Cocky would have felt the same way. He'd always been the one to give a guy an even break and a helping hand, no matter where the guy came from or who his parents were.

I rolled past that diner I'd noticed earlier, and my stomach crooned. My watch told me it was well past midday. I made a U-turn on Douglas and pulled up at the curb. The sign above the door read Curley's Inn. A handwritten sign in the window advertised a bowl of beef stew and a slice of apple pie served with coffee or tea and priced at 30 cents.

A couple of characters in torn clothing loitered on the walk next door to the diner. They caught my eye when I stepped out of my car.

"You fellows hungry?" I said.

They acted surprised. They looked at one another and back at me and nodded. The three of us went inside and settled atop stools at the counter. The waitress approached, and I turned to the men.

"Beef stew and pie?" I said.

"Sounds good," one said.

"It's your nickel," the other one said.

"Beef stew times three," I said to the waitress.

The food arrived, and the men dug in. They weren't chatty. They spooned their stew and forked their pie and nodded thanks when the waitress refilled their coffee cups. I reached into my pocket and retrieved the paper that Ethan had handed me, an article snipped from a teacher's union publication. It included lyrics to a poem by Abel Meeropol, a guy who wrote as Lewis Allan. The poem was titled, "Bitter Fruit." The poet was inspired by a photograph that depicted two Negroes hanging from a tree. They had been lynched in an ordinary town by ordinary citizens, not angry hooligans but everyday folks like those you'd find most anywhere. The mob stood beneath the tree and admired their work. Some smiled. Others pointed. I studied the picture and shuddered. Then I read the poem. I read the poem once, and when I finished, I read it again. The words haunted me.

> *Southern trees bear a strange fruit,*
> *Blood on the leaves and blood at the root,*
> *Black body swinging in the Southern breeze,*
> *Strange fruit hanging from the poplar trees.*

"Did you hear me?" she said.

I glanced toward the voice. The waitress held the coffeepot above my cup.

"I asked if you wanted more coffee."

The men had finished their food, and I was ready to leave.

"No, thanks," I said.

"Will this be together or separate?" she said.

I reached into my pocket and stood up.

"Separate," I said.

The men threw me a look, but I reached out and shook their hands. It gave me a chance to palm a silver dollar to each of them. Each man would pay for his own food. Outside on the walk, one of them spoke.

"That was decent, mister. Who do we owe our thanks to?"

"You can thank Cocky Wright," I said.

They raised their hands and waved.

"Thanks, Mr. Wright," they said.

I touched my fedora and saluted.

"So long, fellas." I said.

7

A man in a blue suit.

Monday, April 25th

The movie at the Miller was *Test Pilot,* and it looked to be a winner, a good story with a terrific cast. I'd promised Lucille a night out, but not long into the movie I realized we'd made a poor choice. That particular film on that particular night proved to be a lousy diversion for a guy looking to dodge thoughts of the aircraft industry for a few hours. The movie brought thoughts of Stearman Aircraft, the meeting with the three stooges, Veatch, Young, and Townsend, and the accusations and suspicions directed toward my pal.

Test Pilot starred Clark Gable, Myrna Loy, and Spencer Tracy. The title was a giveaway, a film involving airplanes, but the top drawer cast swayed me. Stars drew audiences into theaters. I recalled an earlier Gable film, *It Happened One Night,* when he shared the screen with Claudette Colbert. In a memorable scene, Gable demonstrated for Colbert how a man undresses, first the coat, then the tie, then the shirt. Viewers were stunned at the sight of Clark Gable's bare torso. He wasn't wearing an undershirt. Rumor had it that sales of men's undershirts plummeted that year. Movie stars possessed that power. Who knew? Maybe one day a movie star would run for president.

I bought a pair of tickets, and the stars delivered on the silver screen. There was an obligatory romance, and the death of the lead character's best pal hit close to home. Another scene included a baseball game, again reminding me of my pal, and another scene depicted a pilot making an emergency landing in a field somewhere in Kansas. The landscape on the screen brought a smile. The range of hills in the background belonged to a back lot in southern California, not a farm field in Kansas.

The story revolved around America's need to develop military aircraft. It hinted at an impending war and reminded me again of my conversation with Veatch and the federal agents. It was a good film but a lousy diversion, and when the credits started to roll, I stood up and helped Lucille with her wrap. A moment later, we were on the street taking in the evening air.

"That was a quick exit," Lucille said. "Are you okay?"

"I'm fine. The movie conjured up disturbing thoughts, that's all. Hungry?" I said.

"Maybe a little something," she said.

The restaurant at the Eaton Hotel was open and only a few blocks away, so we decided to walk there. We crossed Broadway in front of the theater, and Lucille spent a few moments browsing the window at the J.C. Penney store while I smoked a cigarette. At the corner we walked across Douglas and turned east. We passed by the Lawrence Block building and continued strolling until we reached the Eaton Hotel on the corner at St. Francis.

The lobby was quiet but not empty. A few men, business types, read newspapers and smoked. Inside the restaurant, we took a table near a window that looked onto the sidewalk along Douglas Avenue. Lucille spooned cottage cheese and peaches from a small bowl. The waitress placed a slice of chocolate cake on the table between us, filled our cups with coffee, and edged away. Another couple sat at a table closer to the entrance. A man in a blue suit came in and took a table off to the side. He unfolded a newspaper and turned to the sports page.

"I liked the movie," Lucille said. "Romance, flying, and it had some baseball in it, too. Tell me a baseball story, one about Cocky. You've always said the game brought the two of you together."

I tasted the cake and sipped my coffee. Lucille took a bite of cake, too.

"Baseball was always there, right from the beginning," I said. "We met on a ball field. You know that. We played ball, we watched other teams play, and we followed big league games on the radio. Cocky took after his pop. His dad was a White Sox fan, so he grew up a White Sox fan, too. His dad dreamed of going to Chicago and watching his Sox play in Comiskey Park. Time went by, and that dream faded. Then, when Cocky's dad turned sixty, they threw a party, and Cocky gave him a surprise. He'd scraped together enough money for train tickets to the Windy City. The old man couldn't believe it."

Lucille and I each took another forkful of cake. The waitress refilled our cups.

"They spent four days in the Windy City," I said, "and went to Comiskey Park every day. They watched a series between the White Sox and the St. Louis Browns. The Sox swept the Browns. Won every game. Cocky saw his hero, Eddie Collins, for the first time. Collins played second base. There were other great players back then, Joe Jackson in left, Buck Weaver at third, several good pitchers. They saw them all. They lived on hot dogs, peanuts, and beer. That was their diet, but they feasted on baseball. They came home with empty pockets, fulfilled dreams, and enough memories to ward off a winter chill. Cocky's dad fed on those memories until he passed on three years later. A brain tumor took him. He was around to celebrate when the White Sox won the World Series in 1917, but he died before the scandal. That was two years later."

"I remember that," Lucille said. "It was in the papers. They called it the Black Sox scandal."

I nodded.

"That's right. Cocky said it was the only time he was happy that his dad wasn't alive. It would have killed him. Eight players tossed out of baseball for cheating. They said they rigged the games to lose. That's what they claimed, anyway. Lousy gamblers pulled the strings and paid off the players. One of those players was Joe Jackson, a dumb kid with a truckload of talent, the son of a sharecropper, poor and uneducated. They called him Shoeless Joe, but he could play the game. People still talk about him. He played well that year, too. He always played his best. He led both teams in the Series, had a dozen hits. Buck Weaver, another great one, had eleven hits, but they booted him out, too, along with a half-dozen others. Not Eddie Collins, though. Cocky's hero wasn't banned. His hero was clean. Collins and other innocents on the team came to be known as the Clean Sox. Eddie Collins was Cocky's hero, the man he admired. That's the man Cocky was, too. Clean. Some claim he was dirty, but my pal was clean. I intend to prove it."

"How was he as a player?" she said.

I lit a cigarette and looked over the room. The couple near the door had finished and left. The man in the blue suit drank coffee and smoked. He stared at the newspaper on his table and wrote in a small notebook. The rest of the tables remained empty.

"He was good. He stood out in our corner of the world," I said, "not big but quick on his feet and quick with a bat. He had range and covered a lot of ground. I remember a play he made once, a lefty hitter at the plate and a runner on second. The batter hit a shot up the middle, a line drive over the top of second base. Everyone thought it was a hit. It should have been a hit. The runner on second took off for third, and Cocky sprinted and dove and snagged the ball in the air just inches above the ground. Still on his knees, he reached out and slapped his glove on second base, an unassisted double play. He was good, and fans loved him, but he shrugged it off. He never sought the limelight, but he knew how to play the game."

We finished and stood to leave. I placed Lucille's wrap around her shoulders and glanced at the man in the blue suit. His ashtray was full, and his coffee cup was empty. He hadn't turned a page of his newspaper since he sat down. The waitress brought the coffeepot to his table, but he shook his head.

I settled up the bill, and we moved toward the exit. I opened the door and caught sight of the man in blue reflected in the glass. He had left the restaurant and entered a telephone booth in the lobby. The short hairs on my neck bristled again, but I shrugged it off.

We walked back to my car outside the Miller Theater. We turned onto Douglas and crossed over the river, continuing west until we reached Lucille's place on Clarence. She was tired, and I'd had a long day. Still, we lingered over a goodnight kiss. I squeezed her and held her close and raised an eyebrow. She pecked me on the cheek and whispered, "Incorrigible," in my ear. Then, she smiled and closed her door.

I crossed back over the river and drove north toward a two-story house on Lewellen a couple of blocks west of Waco. I parked at the curb in front and climbed the outside stairs to the second floor, my place. I stood on the landing, hand on the doorknob. Something seemed out of place. The porch light was on, just as I'd left it, but the milk box had moved. It was six or eight inches from its usual spot flush against the house.

The lock on the door showed a number of scratches, probably accumulated over the years I figured. I went inside and turned on a light in the kitchen. The house appeared to be empty. The only sound was the usual chorus of ticking clocks. A quick check of the remaining rooms confirmed that no one was hiding behind a door or in a closet. Everything seemed okay. I poured a shot of bourbon and spotted an open book on the arm of my chair. The book was where I'd left it, but it had been turned upside down.

A closer inspection revealed other things out of place. The Plymouth clock on the mantel had shifted position. I noted a sliver of polished wood next to the clock while the remaining mantel surface had a film of dust. Then I discovered the cracked dome on my Austrian Zappler clock, and I uttered a profanity. Someone had been in my home.

It wasn't the FBI. They had a warrant. They could come through the door anytime they wanted. Someone else had been there. Who? I thought back to the man in blue. Did it have anything to do with the man in blue at the restaurant? Had he followed Lucille and me? After we left, he used the telephone in the lobby. Maybe he called a confederate, alerting him to clear out of my home. Could be, I thought. Or not. Maybe the man in blue was just Joe Schmoe, a regular guy who liked to read the sports page. Maybe I was growing paranoid.

Still, someone had broken into my home. What did I have that everyone wanted? I pondered that, too. I reached into my coat pocket and touched the empty envelope with my name printed across its front. The key Cocky left me was on my keychain. What did the key unlock?

"Talk to me, Cocky," I said.

I listened, but all I got in return was a chorus of ticking clocks.

8
A tall man and
a woman with auburn curls.

Tuesday, April 26th

While my mechanic tinkered beneath the hood of my roadster, I looked over the flier Ethan Alexander had handed me the day before. The Daughters of the American Revolution would host a noon luncheon that day at the Forum. Guests were invited to enjoy a fine meal and hear aspiring politicians deliver brief, "meet the candidate" speeches. Each speaker would be granted five minutes at the podium to introduce himself and his platform. The admission price was fifty cents, a bit steep for a meal, but proceeds would fill the coffers of the Daughters of the American Revolution.

Normally, I avoided get-togethers of that nature. I read the papers and listened to the radio, gathered information, and voted yea or nay. Politicians who postured, posed, and opined didn't appeal to me. I'd rather be staked out beneath the noonday sun than listen to them yammer. Still, Ethan Alexander recommended I attend. He suspected a connection between politics and the German American Bund, and the FBI suspected a connection between the Bund and my pal Cocky. I glanced at my watch and tucked the flier into my pocket.

My mechanic kept a garage next to his home on Oak in the Delano neighborhood west of the ballpark. He knew how to keep my roadster running. He had been employed by The Jones Motor Car Company until a fire destroyed the business. The company built fine automobiles that were popular and sold well, but the fire left them bankrupt, and they closed their doors. My mechanic was out of a job, so he opened his own garage.

I'd inherited my Jones model from a wealthy client. I recovered some stolen jewelry, but when it came time to pay me for my services, the man found himself long on wealth but short on cash. He didn't stiff me. Instead, he offered the roadster in lieu of cash. The car was worth more than my fee, but he insisted, and I accepted. The roadster showed some age, but who didn't? In my eyes, she possessed the beauty and charm of a debutante at a ball.

I lit a cigarette, and we talked baseball while he worked. I knew little about the mechanics of an automobile, but I enjoyed watching a man who knew his job. We hashed over Joe DiMaggio's new contract with the Yankees while he leaned over the fender with his head beneath the hood. Joe D. had held out for forty G's but settled for twenty-five. We discussed overpaid athletes for a few minutes until he declared the job finished and wiped his hands on a grease-stained rag. I paid him, shook his hand, and left.

I had a few minutes to kill before the luncheon began, so I went for a drive. I needed a moment with my thoughts, and I did my best thinking behind the wheel of my roadster. Driving helped me relax. A man can't think if he's not relaxed. Trying too hard or staring too hard at a problem was no way to find a solution. It only led to frustration. Sometimes it was better to look off to the side and let the solution appear. It was like trying to spot that one star in the sky. If you stared right at it, it would fall into your blind spot, and you'd miss it. You had to look to the side and let it appear.

I drove west until I reached the Masonic Home on the southwest corner of Maple and Seneca. Robert Lawrence, city founder, once had a home on that spot. The Masons bought the property before the turn of the century but had to rebuild the structure when the home burned down. Robert Lawrence loved maple trees, and he planted a host of them. Those trees gave the street its name.

I turned north onto Seneca and passed by Tom's Inn but didn't stop. Eight days earlier, Cocky and I sat on barstools at the tavern and toasted the end of the dark season. The next day, his light went out forever. Cocky and I never discussed politics, but we each knew the other's thoughts. I couldn't imagine my friend belonging to an organization like the Bund, not the group that Ethan Alexander had described to me. So, why did the FBI have an interest in Cocky? Someone found photographs in his toolbox after he died. What else did he have that they wanted? Cocky had something to tell me that day at Tom's, but he wanted to tell me at his place. He never got the chance. What did he want to tell me?

I reached McLean Boulevard and dropped south on the winding road that hugged the river. Cocky left a key along with an empty envelope with my name on it. Sundown searched the farm for anything else, but she came up empty, just as I figured she would. Cocky wouldn't hide something near his family, not something that others were after. He wouldn't put his family in harm's way. Whatever he had was hidden someplace else. I had to figure out where that place was.

I slowed down when I passed by Lawrence Stadium. It stood quiet and empty, pennants flying high overhead. There was no game scheduled for that day, but there would be one on another day soon. There would be baseball. There would always be baseball.

I crossed the river and drove downtown. Traffic grew heavier as I approached the Forum on South Water between William and English. Parking was limited nearby the auditorium, so I circled the block and found a spot along the curb two blocks east on Market. I stepped onto the sidewalk and fell in with other pedestrians headed the same direction.

The Wichita Forum had grown in a quarter of a century. It held major community events, expositions, plays and movies, concerts, and welcomed other large gatherings. A sizable crowd milled on the steps and flowed inside.

A taxicab pulled up and double-parked in front of the entrance. A tall, slender man in his thirties exited the vehicle and buttoned his tailored suit coat. He smoothed his dark hair with one hand and surveyed the crowd. His expression revealed little interest in the people around him. He stuck his head back inside the cab and spoke in a loud voice.

"I'm late," he said.

He stood erect and walked away without a backward glance. His eyes focused on the door, and his height allowed him to ignore the heads in front of him. He walked through the crowd as if it didn't exist and elbowed his way into the building.

I looked back at the cab idling in the street. High heels and slender legs exited from the rear seat, followed by a woman wearing a blue dress and auburn curls. She rose and watched her companion disappear. I watched her watch him. The woman was stunning. Just for a moment, I wondered how a warm blooded male could turn his back on a woman so beautiful. Then, I forgot about him and studied her.

Her ice blue eyes matched her dress. Her profile revealed a delicate jaw and slender neck. The auburn curls fell to her shoulders. Even when those shoulder slumped, I couldn't take my eyes off of her. She opened her purse and forked over a bill to the cabbie. She did not look at the cabbie or acknowledge his thanks as she stepped onto the sidewalk.

I fell in beside her and said something witty and charming about the weather. Her ice blue eyes glanced my way for a fraction of a second. We climbed the steps together, and when we reached the door, I doffed my fedora and stepped aside to allow her entrance. Those eyes delivered a quizzical look, and she raised an eyebrow a fraction of an inch.

"Thank you," she said.

She entered and turned her back on me as she moved toward the tables at the front of the room. I remained at the rear of the room and watched her walk away. Just for a moment I gave my imagination free rein. Another time, another place, I thought to myself before coming back to the present.

The meeting hall was decked out in patriotic colors. Red, white, and blue bunting hung from the rafters and draped long tables arranged for the banquet. Other people edged toward the front, but I chose a seat near the rear and close to the doorway. I wanted to observe the crowd while the candidates spoke. Citizens of the Sunflower State would vote for a governor and a senator that November. State representatives also sought seats, as did Wichita's mayor and several council members.

I settled into a chair at a rear table. A dowager took the chair to my right, and a heavyset man in a snug suit plopped down in the chair to my left. He looked my way and flashed a toothy grin.

"Do you mind if I join you?" he said.

His smile suggested he'd just met his new best friend.

"Allow me to introduce myself," he said.

He gave me his name and held out a business card clasped between a pair of sausages that resembled a thumb and a forefinger. I read the card, Midwest Mutual Life Insurance. I raised my eyebrows and returned his smile. The man grew encouraged.

"You look like a successful man," he said. "I'll wager you're a businessman. Am I right? A man looking for a secure future, a future for you and your family. Am I right? I'll bet you have a lovely missus and a passel of little ones at home, too. Huh? Am I right?"

I said nothing, but he wasn't put off. He continued.

"We at Midwest Mutual are on the lookout for men like yourself, responsible men, men who value their loved ones and wish to protect them against the uncertainties and vagaries of fate.

One must insure himself to protect those he loves, to hold the ravages of poverty at bay, especially during these perilous economic times."

He'd memorized the script and rehearsed it. He beamed, and I nodded and smiled.

"Brother, you're just the guy I've been looking for," I said.

His smile grew larger, a seeming impossibility.

"Other agents won't talk to me," I said. "It's discouraging. They're all too nervous, I guess, but what do doctors know, anyway? I think those doctors are full of hooey, don't you? They give me six months to live, but what do they know, huh? The lousy bums and their lousy tests. Then again, they could be right. You never know. What did you call it? The uncertainties and vagaries of fate? You hammered the nail, fella, right on the head. That's good stuff. You're right. We couldn't have met at a better time. Where do I sign?"

I paused and pulled out my handkerchief and coughed into it. The man's eyes grew wide. His mouth remained open, but his smile disappeared. He edged back like he was sitting next to Typhoid Mary. For all he knew, he was. He couldn't tell if I was lying or telling the truth. At that point, it didn't matter. We both knew I'd never earn a coveted position in his company's actuarial tables. Our brief friendship came to an abrupt halt. He muttered an apology and snatched his business card from my hand. He stood up and moved away. Further down the long table he took another chair beside his next target. I had to give him credit for resilience. He shook off our conversation and directed his attention to his newest best friend.

The elderly woman to my right looked down into her lap and shook her head. She wore a print dress and blue hair. She stifled a chuckle with her handkerchief.

"Don't laugh," I said. "You're sitting next to a dying man here."

Her chuckle gave way to honest laughter.

"Careful, lady," I said. "I'm drawn to women who laugh at my jokes."

She shook her head again and sighed.

"Your behavior is atrocious," she said, "and I'm twenty years your senior. Has any woman ever told you that you're incorrigible?"

"Strangely enough she has. Recently in fact."

That really got the old gal. She laughed again, out loud this time, and I smiled back at her. A tap on a microphone brought the crowd's attention to the podium at the front of the room. A woman in a brown dress and matching hat spoke into the microphone. She introduced herself as the DAR president of the local chapter. She encouraged the people still mingling to move to their tables. The crowd rose when a man in a clerical collar offered a prayer and remained standing while we sang the national anthem.

Young men and women dressed in white shirts and black slacks or skirts began serving meals, and the chapter president introduced the first speaker. Servers moved along the tables carrying plates of sliced roast beef, mashed potatoes, green beans, and dinner rolls. The food looked better on the menu than it tasted at the table. It probably had a fighting chance at being edible when it left the kitchen, but by the time it reached the tables, entrées had cooled and vegetables had gone soggy. I toyed with a few bites and rested my fork next to the plate. A scoop of vanilla ice cream followed the main course, but I settled on coffee and lit a cigarette.

Candidates drew lots and took the microphone in turn. They spoke while the audience dined. Speakers contended with clicking flatware, clacking porcelain, and divided attentions. Candidates not at the microphone sat at a table that faced the audience, each one eager to convince voters that he was the best candidate for the office he sought. Each man, one after the other, proved to be as appealing as the scoop of ice cream melting in my bowl.

Candidates for local offices promised school improvements and safe streets. Candidates for state offices vowed lower taxes and increased benefits. Not one candidate offered a clue as to how lower taxes would pay for those additional benefits. They'd leave that to the bean counters. Each speaker held forth for five minutes, then a bell tinkled and the speaker ceded the microphone to the next in line.

The chapter president introduced a candidate, and the name caught my attention. Alfred Warren was running for U. S. Senate. He was also one of the men Ethan Alexander had mentioned to me. His brand of politics was not far removed from the ideology espoused by the German American Bund. He defended racial segregation and spoke out against Jewish bankers who controlled the economy. He had other thoughts fueled by hatred. For a preacher, he had a harsh way of dealing with folks he didn't like, but he dealt in rooting out evil and left it to others to forgive and forget.

As he spoke, young people moved between the tables and handed out copies of *Spotlight*, the newspaper published by Raymond Tipple. Tipple supported Warren and fed from the same trough. His newspaper was the print form of what we heard. The bell rang on Warren, and he exited the building with an entourage in his wake.

I glanced at my watch and scanned the room. Others in the crowd shifted in their seats and looked at their watches. Most were expected to return to desks or retail counters following their lunch hour.

A final candidate moved to the microphone, the tall man who had left his beautiful companion alone in the cab. He approached the microphone, surveyed the audience, and said nothing. He remained silent and looked at the crowd. It seemed an odd ploy for a man granted only a few minutes to tell his story, but the man knew what he was doing. The silence was deafening. He directed his gaze from one side of the room to the other. The click and clack of porcelain and flatware went silent. Murmurs ceased. Without uttering a word, he captured the crowd. When he spoke, his voice was severe and humorless.

"Enough," he said, "Enough with New Deals. Enough with Communism. Enough with taxes, with taking your money, money you worked to earn, so bureaucrats in Washington could dole it out willy-nilly to this bum or that bum. Enough. I am running for Congress. I will root out the Communists, the scoundrels who have infiltrated our government, the thieves who take your hard-earned money. Change is coming, and I represent that change."

People looked at one another. Some heads shook no. Other heads went up and down. Everyone listened.

"I vow to fight and vote against every bill that comes from the Jew sympathizer occupying the White House."

Some people gasped. Some mumbled. There was scattered applause.

"I vow to fight for American ideals, the values we hold dear."

The bell tinkled, and he went silent but didn't move. He glared at the audience. The chapter president of the DAR stepped to the microphone and thanked everyone for attending. She said something about upcoming events, but no one heard her. No one paid attention. People rose from their chairs, and their voices rose with them. Some people argued with tablemates. Faces grinned, and faces registered disgust. Some loved what the man said. Others hated it. The man had divided the room, but he had captured their attention.

People headed for the exits, and I worked my way to the front where a cluster of people surrounded the tall man. I spotted the woman in the blue dress and auburn curls. She sat at a table to the side and sipped from her cup, unmoved by the hubbub her companion had created. Several young men in suits snaked through the crowd and handed out envelopes, but not to everyone. The recipients they selected were dressed like bank presidents. I caught one of them by the elbow.

"I'll take one," I said.

The young man's eyes went down to my scuffed shoes and traveled up my off-the-rack suit until they reached my fedora. His expression told me I didn't pass muster.

"I don't think so," he said. "This isn't for you."

"So, who's it for?" I said.

"This is an invitation to a private party," he said. "Invited attendees are expected to provide support for our candidate, monetary support. You understand. No offense."

"None taken," I said, a lie. The way he put it would have offended any Schmoe. "I'm not asking for myself. It's for my uncle, but you probably wouldn't like him either. His clothes are usually stained, with oil."

"Oh?" he said.

"Yeah, he was called away on an emergency, so he sent me here in his place. One of his wells brought in a gusher."

The guy looked doubtful, but the lie tripped off my tongue. The two-bit bum wouldn't miss a chance to fleece a fat cat, even one with stains on his clothes. He relinquished an invitation and moved on.

I turned to leave and caught the profile of a man I'd seen before. He was walking toward an exit. It was the man in the blue suit from the Eaton Hotel, the guy who pored over the sports page at the restaurant. He wore a gray suit that day, but it was the same man. The main exit was crowded, so the man moved toward doors at the end of the hall. I followed him through the crowd. He reached the doors and exited. I reached the door and stepped onto the landing a moment later. I scanned the sidewalk and the street. I caught a glimpse as the man climbed into a black sedan down the block. I watched as the car pulled away from the curb and disappeared into the traffic.

9
He lied to me.

Wednesday, April 27th

The next day I went for a drive in the country. Only four days had passed since the funeral and my visit with Sundown on that same day, but I'd grown nervous since then. I couldn't shake the feeling that someone was shadowing me. Maybe someone was watching Sundown, too. I'd feel better if I knew she was safe.

I drove with the top up on the roadster to ward off a chill in the air, but the skies were blue, and the countryside green. Shoots of winter wheat cropped up in the fields. A meadowlark warbled on a fencepost. Another fencepost beyond had an upside down boot resting atop it. Some folks called it a welcome sign, but others called it a warning, a signal to hunters to stay off the land. Some said a wife put her husband's worn-out boots on a post to force him to buy another pair. Others believed it was done in memory of a favorite horse, and still others said it marked a trail for driving cattle. Take your pick, I figured. An upside down boot on a fencepost meant most anything.

Down the road, a board leaned against a fence. It bore a carved letter X inside a circle. A hobo had placed the board there, a sign that he'd gotten a handout at the house, food most likely. Hoboes had their own dictionary of signs and symbols intended for fellow travelers, such as a warning to avoid a farm, or watch for the dog, or don't drink the water.

The farms were family operations, small enough to be worked by the family and large enough to provide for them all. Some prospered. Others didn't. At the correction line south of Sundown's place, I took the jog in the road and passed by the old Miller place. The bank had foreclosed on the Miller's in the early thirties. The house and barn remained empty, and the fields lay fallow. Someone said the old man's heart gave out, and the widow moved into town to live with a spinster daughter. Nothing remained of the farm but weathered buildings, ghosts, and memories.

Two miles later, my roadster rolled over a culvert and onto Sundown's place. Sissy the collie wagged her tail and barked my arrival. Sundown stood on the walk next to the gate and visited with another woman. They both turned my way, and Sundown waved. The other woman gave Sundown a brief hug and climbed into a dusty Chevy. I got out of my car, and the woman nodded through the windshield as she drove away. Sundown shushed the dog, and I scratched the dog behind the ear.

"What brings you out this way?" Sundown said. "Not that I'm ungrateful for the company, mind you. Come in, and I'll pour us a cup."

We moved inside to the kitchen table. I noted again the curled wallpaper and the bucket beneath the water stain on the ceiling. I wondered why Cocky had neglected the upkeep of his home. Sundown poured coffee into a pair of cups and offered a slice of coffeecake. I accepted the coffee but declined the cake. She forked a small bite, and I lit a cigarette. She looked at me and put down her fork.

"Normally I'd welcome a social call," she said, "but I didn't just fall off the turnip truck. Times aren't normal, and this isn't a social call. What's up?"

I told Sundown about meeting the FBI agents, first in my office and later with Gordon Veatch. I told her what I knew about the German American Bund, their ideology and beliefs, and I told her about Cocky's alleged involvement. I didn't mention the photographs they found in Cocky's toolbox at Stearman. However, I did tell her that someone had broken into my home.

"I worry about your safety, Sundown. Someone wants something that Cocky had. What that is, I don't know. Have you found anything?"

She shook her head.

"No, not a thing," she said, "and I've searched the place. How about that key? That key must be important. Any idea what it opens?"

"No I don't. Look, I'm not trying to frighten you," I said, "but you've already dealt with one unwelcome visitor, and I'm worried that someone else may show up. Has anyone else visited you since the funeral?"

"Just neighbors and a friend or two from town. Gals I used to see every day."

Sundown's reference was to women she once lived with in the two-story house on the edge of town.

"The woman who just left," I said, "a neighbor?"

She nodded.

"Imogene," she said. "She and her husband raised four children. They have a farm down by the river."

Sundown swept a faded dishtowel across her eyes.

"She's more than a neighbor. She's a dear friend. We almost lost them some years ago. They were ready to quit. The river flooded. The water swole up out of its banks and poured over their land. It left the house standing, but it didn't spare their crops. They had nothing to harvest that year and precious little to feed their children, larder all but empty, and no money to buy food. They were ready to give up and move on, but Cocky wouldn't have it. He had to help. He devised a plan and told me to invite them over for dinner. They came on a Sunday, Imogene and Alfred and the four young ones. After our meal, Cocky and Alfred went out onto the porch and smoked tobacco. Imogene and I didn't know what they were talking about. We only heard their voices when they raised them, and when they raised them it was mostly Alfred's voice we heard. He objected to what Cocky had to say, but they kept at it, and eventually their voices quieted. Soon after, the men came back inside.

"They'd struck a deal. Alfred's family would share our crop that year, fifty-fifty right down the middle. We'd have less to live on for a year, but we'd make it. Alfred looked on it as charity, and that's what he objected to, but Cocky said it wasn't charity. The agreement was to share the harvest if one family had a bad year. Cocky explained that if a drought came along and our crops failed, Alfred's bottomland near the river would produce. Alfred would share his crop that year, fifty-fifty. It was an insurance policy against the whims of nature, one neighbor helping the other. The men shook hands on it, and that was that. It was settled.

"It worked out well. We've had good harvests and bad harvests, but we've managed. That summer of '36 hit us hard, though. It wiped out our crops. Awful dust storms blew in, and locusts came, too. The rains didn't come, but Alfred's bottomland did fine. By then, of course, Cocky was working for Cessna, and we had steady income to tide us over. We didn't rely solely on our crops to survive. That didn't matter to Alfred. Our crops failed, and he split his harvest with us, fifty-fifty."

Sundown wiped her eyes again.

"Imogene stopped to see how I was getting along. She told me that nothing will change in our agreement now that Cocky is gone. Our agreement still stands."

She refilled our cups.

"I didn't mean to go on," she said. "My mind has dredged up memories this week. Back to your question. No more strangers have been by to see me, just friends."

Debbie Lynn came into the kitchen carrying little Cindy in her arms.

"I heard a piece of what you were talking about," she said. "Are we in any danger?"

Sundown took the baby and cooed at her. Debbie Lynn retrieved her jar of Mentholatum from a pocket and dabbed some on her chapped lips. The young woman looked wan and drawn, but she'd traded the threadbare linsey-woolsey dress she wore on my last visit for a yellow dress Lucille had given her, and it fit her well.

"That's why I stopped by," I said, "to make sure you're not in danger."

"That's right nice," she said, "and we appreciate it, but what about after you leave? Then what? You can't be here all the time."

She had me there.

"Did Cocky talk about work much?" I said. "What did he say about his job, the men he worked with?"

"He never said much," Sundown said. "He didn't complain, if that's what you mean. He liked his work, being a mechanic. It suited him."

"How about the other men? Did he talk about them?"

"He got along," Sundown said. "His boss gave him a job and let him do it. Cocky liked that. He didn't hang over his shoulder and tell him how he wanted it done. He left him alone to do his work."

"And the other men?" I said. "Did he make friends, or enemies?"

"No one that he mentioned. He hadn't worked there long, you know. He wasn't there a year. He never brought anybody to the farm, anyway. I think he got along with the other men. He looked forward to his work every day."

Debbie Lynn chimed in.

"There was one guy. Dad mentioned his name one time. He didn't say anything bad about him, really, just the tone of his voice. You could tell he didn't think much of him."

"Do you remember his name?"

She thought for a moment.

"He used a nickname. Something like Charlie, but that wasn't it. Choppy maybe, but that doesn't sound right either. Dad didn't say anything bad about him. I could just tell he didn't think much of him."

The baby fussed, and Debbie Lynn reached for her and left the kitchen. I had more questions for Sundown.

"The feds draw a connection between the German American Bund and certain politicians running for office this year. They've asked me about Cocky's political leanings, and my answer to them was I haven't the slightest idea. We never discussed it. What can you tell me? Was Cocky involved with this Bund?"

"Cocky wouldn't have joined a group like the one you described. He never hated other people," she said. "You know that."

"Yes, I do know that," I said. "He'd never single out a group, Negroes, Jews, or anyone else for persecution. He gave every man a fair shot."

She smiled.

"Do you remember the House of David?" she said. "I apologize. Another memory."

I raised an eyebrow.

"The House of David? That was years before you and Cocky were married. We were youngsters then."

"Yes, but he told me stories. Something you said dredged up a memory. He talked about that team and when you played baseball against them."

"They were good, better than we were. They wiped up the field with us. We didn't stand a chance. I don't remember why they bothered to play us at all."

"They played against you because that was the only game they could get," Sundown said. "That's the way Cocky told it."

The House of David was a traveling baseball team, barnstorming members of a religious cult. They played well, but they weren't always welcomed by the local citizens. Hulking men with thick beards intimidated some folks and frightened others. Some communities wouldn't give them a game or human civility, either. They didn't always find room and board. They often lacked clean sheets and indoor plumbing. Their hygiene was iffy.

"Cocky arranged a game between our teams," I said, "but we didn't give them much of a game."

"Those were Cocky's words," she said, "but those men liked playing here. They weren't ready to leave. They wanted to stay in Wichita for a while and play other teams. After they whipped you fellas, Cocky talked to them, got to know them. They had a team lined up to play against them, Negroes from Oklahoma, and they arranged to play games in Lawrence Stadium. The problem was, they couldn't find a place that would put them up. They needed beds and food, but no hotel would have them. They all said the same thing. 'Cult members and Negroes under our roof? Not here.' That's when Cocky got involved."

"He never told me this," I said.

"He wouldn't have. He never crowed about the things he did. Cocky visited one hotel after another and heard the same story again and again. Not interested. Well, a more stubborn man you never met. He found a hotel, not in the best neighborhood, but decent accommodations. The owner was reluctant to give them rooms, but the team manager hauled a wad of greenbacks out of his pocket, and the owner went weak in the knees. He couldn't pass up that cash. The hotel had enough beds for everyone if they agreed to double up. For that bunch a bed was a bed, and sleeping with another man didn't make no never mind to them. The hotel had a restaurant, so they were set, the lot of them. The team manager was grateful to Cocky for his help and wanted to pay him something for his trouble. Cocky wouldn't take their money, but he did accept game tickets."

"He took me to those games," I said.

"That was Cocky. Something you said about that German

American Bund brought back those memories. Do you believe a man like the one we knew would belong to an organization that looked down on Jews and Negroes?"

"You know I don't," I said. "How about politics? Was he involved with politicians?"

"No. He never talked about politics, but . . ."

Her voice trailed off, and her eyes focused on something only she could see. I waited. She brought her eyes back to me and continued.

"There is something that doesn't figure. Cocky began working longer hours several weeks before he died. He came home late, and he came home tired. Look at this place. He promised a new roof this spring, but he never got around to it. He stopped fixing up other things around here, too. He never found the time. He worked hard, but something doesn't add up."

She paused again, and I remained silent.

"Cocky brought his paychecks home and gave them to me," she said. "I managed the finances. I put his checks in the bank, and I made sure the bills were paid. The thing is, after Cocky started working all those extra hours, his paycheck never grew. It stayed the same, week after week, the same amount within a dollar or so. It never changed."

A tear fell onto her cheek, and she brushed it away with the dishtowel.

"I didn't ask him about it, but what he did tell me wasn't the truth. He couldn't have been working overtime. He stayed out late and came home tired, but he didn't work more hours, not at Stearman he didn't. He lied to me, Pete. I don't know why, but he lied to me. I can't tell you where he went, and I don't know what he did on those nights. All I know is he wasn't working late at Stearman, and he wasn't at home with me."

10

An investigation, a glare, and a bear.

Wednesday, April 27th

I had no appointment to see Veatch, and I didn't want one. I arrived unannounced. My intent was to catch him off guard, to question him alone without the presence or knowledge of the FBI, or anyone else for that matter.

Blue and yellow biplanes circled overhead as they had done on my last visit to Stearman Aircraft. I parked my roadster and entered the offices adjacent to the hangar. Veatch's secretary, Mrs. Richeson, sat at a typewriter and pecked at the keys. She paused when I walked in and greeted me with a stare. I moved toward Veatch's door, and her stare became a glare. She jumped to her feet.

"Mr. Stone, where do you think you're going? You can't just barge in here."

I cut her off with a look and pointed a finger.

"No phone calls, no interruptions," I said.

Her eyes grew wide, and her hand went to her throat. She looked at me, mouth agape, and plopped down hard onto her chair. I opened the door to Veatch's office and went in. I figured I'd find him at his desk, and I was right. He sat with his sleeves rolled to the elbows, a cigar stub in his mouth and a coffee stain on his white shirt. The stain and the stub had probably been there since early that morning. He looked like a man who spent his days moving from his desk to his drafting table and back again. He removed the stub from his mouth and eyeballed me as I pulled up a chair. I removed my fedora and sat down.

"I didn't know we had an appointment," he said.

"We don't. I want to talk to you alone—without the Katzenjammer kids listening and throwing their two bits in. Just you and me. The FBI has spoken to me. They ask questions. You have questions, I have questions. Everyone has questions. I want some answers."

"We all want answers, Stone. What makes you so special?"

"Not a thing. I'm not special, but Cocky Wright was special. He was one of a kind, and he deserves more respect than he's getting. He deserves to have a guy in his corner. That guy is yours truly. I spoke to his widow this morning. She told me something troubling, so I came here to see you. She told me that Cocky worked late in the weeks before he died. He put in extra hours on the job. That's what he told her, but she has her doubts. She wonders if he really was working overtime. How about it? Was his crew putting in more time recently? You've mentioned the Boeing merger. Does that play into working longer hours?"

"I haven't the slightest idea how many hours Wright worked," he said. "That's a question for his supervisor, not me. Wright didn't work for me. Maybe the widow is right. Maybe he had other reasons for coming home late."

"If he did, they were good reasons, and I intend to find out what they were. I'll be talking to his supervisor, too, but before I do I have a question for you. Give me the straight dope, Gordon. Do you think Cocky was involved in anything illegal, anything that could bring harm to Stearman? Forget about the FBI and their suspicions. I'm asking you. Do you question his loyalty to the company?"

"Frankly, I don't know what to believe," he said, "and don't think it hasn't been on my mind. It would have been out of character for Wright to behave in such a way. I always thought of him as an upstanding man, a fine addition to the company. You're right about one thing, though. The FBI suspects Wright of taking those pictures. Don't forget, they found them in his toolbox. They suspect others, too. That's their way. The FBI suspects everyone is guilty of something, even you. And what about you? You're the one who recommended Wright to Stearman in the first place. Maybe you're the bad guy. Maybe you're the ringleader and set up the whole shebang. Maybe you're the guy the FBI should be investigating."

I stared at Veatch, and he shook his head. His statement was absurd, and he knew it.

"You know better than that," I said. "You know I'm not involved, and you know Cocky Wright was a standup fellow, a square john. Hoover's boys have you jumping at your own shadow. For the record, the FBI didn't find those pictures. A Stearman employee found them in Cocky's toolbox, your words. They could have been planted by someone else."

Veatch held a match to the stub in his mouth. It failed to light, so he tossed it into an ashtray. He retrieved a fresh cigar from a desk drawer and buzzed the intercom without speaking. A moment later, Mrs. Richeson came in with a grim expression on her face and two cups of coffee in her hands. She placed the coffee on the desk. Veatch thanked her, and she nodded without changing her expression. She ignored me and walked out.

"I don't think your secretary likes me," I said.

"You're too touchy," Veatch said. "Lots of people don't like you."

I shrugged, and he laughed. He lit his fresh cigar, and I lit a cigarette.

"Tell me what you know," he said, "and I'll tell you what I know. Nothing we say leaves the room. Fair enough? I'm fed up with the FBI, too, but if they find out we've talked, they'll put me under a hot lamp. I don't need the aggravation."

"Fair enough, but what I know isn't much. Cocky and your

pilot died in an airplane accident, but after your explanation of what caused the crash, I wonder if it was an accident at all. Were the elevators rigged to fail? I have no proof, and I take it you don't either, but I don't like the way it smells. Someone is after something Cocky had, if he had anything at all. Maybe someone wanted Cocky out of the way. If so, why? After he died, a man from out of town tried to brace Cocky's widow. He showed up at the farm, but he didn't get what he came for."

"Who was it?"

"I have no idea who he was. I never met him, and I never will. He drove a Ford automobile with Michigan plates. I've done some checking on the German American Bund, and their leader, Fritz Kuhn, is out of Detroit. He worked for Ford Motor Company. Maybe there's a connection between the Bund and the man who showed up at the farm. I don't know. I do know that Kuhn is a snake, and so was this mysterious visitor. Maybe they slithered out of the same nest."

"You say you never met this man and you never will. Why not? Maybe you should find him. If you talked to him, you might get some answers."

I shook my head.

"He's out of the picture. He's gone for good, not by my hand, but he's gone."

Veatch pursed his lips and nodded.

"Okay. Is that all?"

"That's all I know. Someone I trust suggested I look for connections between the Bund and local politicians. Maybe Cocky was onto something from that angle, but for now that's just speculation."

I didn't mention the empty envelope or the key Cocky had left behind. There was nothing there for Veatch. I wasn't sure if the envelope and key meant anything at all.

"It was an accident, but it bothers me, too," Veatch said. "The pilot was experienced, and the plane shouldn't have failed. That said, I can't imagine anyone killing two men intentionally for no apparent reason. Where was the motive? If someone wanted Wright out of the picture that raises more questions than it answers."

He knocked the ash off of his cigar into the tray.

"Some weeks ago, Wright came to see me. He brought concerns about the activities of one of his coworkers." Veatch paused. He held his cigar in one hand and drummed the fingers of his other hand on the desk. His eyes held mine when he continued.

"Wright observed a man snapping pictures of devices inside of our airplanes, new technologies that we're developing. This man's behavior was out of line. He had no reason to take pictures of our aircraft, especially their inner workings. Information of that nature is sensitive and secret. Our engineering department and the prototypes we have in development are key reasons Boeing took an interest in us in the first place, why they want Stearman to be a part of their organization. Wright didn't know the man's motivations, so he brought his concern to me."

"That should tell you something about the man," I said. "Cocky was on the up and up, so he came to you. Why did he come to you, though? He worked in another department. He was a mechanic, not an engineer. Why didn't he take this to his supervisor?"

Veatch said nothing, and his eyes never wavered. His silence and his look gave me the answer.

"Because it was his supervisor who took the pictures," I said.

"That's what Wright claimed, anyway. His supervisor took the photographs."

"Something doesn't add up," I said. "You and the FBI fed me a cockamamie story. You suspected my pal was associated with the German American Bund and that he dealt in sensitive photographs. Now you're telling me that Cocky's boss took the pictures."

He shook his head.

"That's not what I said, Pete. I said that Wright claimed his boss took the pictures. He had no proof to back up that claim. He had no photographs, no evidence, just his word. His supervisor denied everything, of course, so we investigated. We grilled other employees in the department and searched personal effects. The investigation was ongoing when Wright died."

"So, my pal comes to you with information about an employee behaving suspiciously, and you investigated. Now he's dead and can't speak for himself, so he takes the heat. Is that it?"

"It's still under investigation," he said again. "The higher ups brought in the FBI. The FBI questioned Wright, and they questioned Pettigrew. That's his supervisor, Darnell Pettigrew. Pettigrew denied everything and said he was innocent. What else would you expect him to say under the circumstances?"

"What has the FBI learned?"

"Not much more than we discovered on our own, at least not as far as I know. They don't report to me. None of the employees knows anything about Wright's claims. No one saw Pettigrew take pictures. Most of these men have worked with Pettigrew for years. They back him up. Maybe Wright told the truth, maybe not, but until recently we had two men pointing fingers at each other. Meanwhile, we're negotiating a merger with Boeing. The deal will be complete in a few weeks. The last thing Boeing wants to do is to bring a cancer into the fold."

"You didn't fire Wright or Pettigrew," I said. "Why not, considering your deal with Boeing?"

"Fire them for what? We had no evidence of any wrongdoing, at least we didn't until Wright died. Oh, the honchos thought about letting them go, sweeping it under the rug, but I persuaded them to wait. They both deserved a fair shake until we had answers."

"Do you believe Cocky told the truth?"

"I believe we owed him the benefit of the doubt. We still do. What kind of man would yell 'Fire!' and then leave the matches where anyone can find them? It makes no sense. Why would Wright warn me about those pictures and then hide them in his toolbox?"

"And Pettigrew?"

"Pettigrew is still on the job. All we have against him is what Wright told me. They've found nothing to implicate Pettigrew, no evidence of wrongdoing on his part. So, Pettigrew still works for us."

There wasn't much else to discuss. We'd each learned what the other knew, and Veatch had smoked his cigar to a stub. We said our goodbyes, and I left and closed the door. Outside of his office, Mrs. Richeson stood next to an open file cabinet. I walked by her and flashed a smile. She replied with a cool look. I wanted to make amends for my gruff behavior.

"Say, I apologize for being abrupt earlier," I said. "I've had a bad day. It must be the lousy weather."

She glanced out a window. The sky was blue and clear. Sunshine filled the room.

"Tell you what," I said. "Just to show you my heart is in the right place, why don't you take the rest of the day off? My treat. I'll clear it with your boss."

The clock on the wall said four-thirty. Her day's work would end in a half hour. She glared at me and removed a file from the cabinet. She sat down at her desk and continued to glare at me. I winked at her. She raised her eyebrows and shook her head, but her glare softened. The corners of her mouth twitched upward a bit. I tapped my fedora, flashed my pearly whites, and left.

I got into my car and thought about my conversation with Veatch for a moment. The doors to the hangar stood open. The day was winding down, but several workers remained inside the hangar. No blue and yellow Kaydet Trainers flew overhead, and no men with clipboards could be seen. The heavyset man who inspected the planes on my earlier visit drove off in a sedan. I got out of my roadster and walked toward the hangar. As long as I was there, I might as well stir the hornet's nest.

Workers hustled to finish their day, gathering, sorting, and packing materials, some of it to be moved to a Boeing facility no doubt. A tall man carried a clipboard in one hand, a pencil in the other hand, and a layer of flab around his middle. He wore pressed khakis and a shiny helmet and looked like a stranger to heavy lifting. The name 'Chappie' was stitched above a pocket on his shirt. That must have been the name Debbie Lynn tried to recall when I visited the farm. He walked my way, and I asked him if Pettigrew was around. He said no and kept walking. I stepped in front of him.

"Not so fast," I said. "Where can I find Pettigrew?"

"I told you he's not here," he said. "Come back another time."

The guy had swagger and little time to waste on me. A clipboard and a shiny helmet will do that to a guy. He was built like a bear, and possessed a similar disposition.

"Chappie, that's your name? I know he's not here, Chappie. You already told me that. So, if he isn't here, where can I find him?"

He shook his head like I must be deaf and dumb.

"I told you to try another time. He's not here."

"I know he's not here. We've established that. He must be someplace else. Everybody is someplace, Chappie. So, where's Pettigrew?"

Poking a bear with a stick was a weakness of mine. I've had the weakness all my life and never really tried to overcome it. Chappie stepped closer, and I raised my eyes to meet his. He looked upset. That wasn't a good thing.

"You better leave, mister," he said. "You don't belong here. If I have to show you the exit, it'll be with the toe of my boot."

"No reason to get hostile, Chappie," I said and handed him my card. "Give this to Pettigrew when he's no longer missing in action. Tell him I was asking after him, will you? Tell him I'd like to get my picture taken and I understand he's the fellow to see. I was told he has a camera. Can you remember all that?"

He glanced at my card.

"A gumshoe. I might have known."

"Good for you, Chappie. You can read. I thought that clipboard might be a prop."

"Get out."

The bear was riled. He was no longer entertained by my presence. I touched the brim of my fedora and got out.

11
A man named Richter
And a man named Bernstein.

Thursday, April 28th

The room atop the Hotel Lassen was tricked in intimacy and elegance. Window drapes of rich velvet in deep maroon shielded guests from the distractions of city lights. Wool carpet in a lighter maroon dampened noise from the floors below. An array of Art Deco club chairs upholstered in grain leather comforted guests. Walnut serving tables near the drapes held silver tureens piled with shrimp on ice. Crystal bowls of black and scarlet caviar were perched alongside saucers of toast sliced into points. On another table, flutes of champagne sparkled in the subdued lighting. Slender tapers in silver candlesticks flickered throughout the room, their soft glow enhanced by Art Deco lamps crafted from cut glass and trimmed in gold.

I sipped champagne and thumbed the invitation I'd finagled from the aide at the Forum. The private meeting was intended for a select group of gentlemen, gentlemen of status and from a certain class. In other words, suckers with a lot of dough. I didn't fit the profile. All I lacked were status, class, and dough.

I took a chair in the corner at the back of the room and nodded hello to a gentleman who was seated nearby. He returned a cursory glance and a curt nod and swiveled his chair to face the other direction. I was not offended. The back of his head was every bit as interesting as his face.

Attendees entered the room and drifted towards the tables of appetizers and champagne. They filled plates with generous portions of delicacies, guzzled flutes of bubbly, and struck up animated conversations with country club acquaintances, everyone cozy and nice. All were male, dressed in dark suits, and had heads of gray or pink depending on how much of their hair remained. They smelled of tobacco, fine cologne, and money, lots of it. No one took notice of me or spoke to me, which suited me fine. Money gave those who had it the privilege of ignoring those who didn't. I sat among the stuffed shirts and fat wallets and looked as proper and in place as a bug on a windshield.

A few chairs remained empty when a trio of men entered the room. All three were familiar to me, two by name, and the third I'd seen. FBI agent Leonard Young and his partner, George Townsend, walked in with another man trailing behind. I'd seen the man on two previous occasions, at the Eaton restaurant when he wore a blue suit and again at the Forum when he was dressed in gray. His name was unknown to me, and his connection to the FBI added to the mystery. They took chairs near the front of the room.

At eight o'clock on the dot, a tall, slender man came through the door with a pair of aides at his heels. The man who had cast a spell over the audience at the Forum wore a broad grin beneath cold, dark eyes. He crossed the floor with long strides, pausing to shake hands extended from chairs as he went by. His aides refreshed empty flutes with more champagne.

The man of the hour, decked out in a navy pinstriped suit, burgundy tie, and matching pocket square, cut a striking figure. His dark hair was slicked back, not a strand out of place. He moved forward and assumed a stance near the front of the room that allowed him to see each person seated, and it allowed each person to see him. He glanced at his reflection in a gilt-edged mirror, turned to the audience, and spoke in a strong, clear voice. As he spoke, he looked into the eyes of each man, one after the other, until he made eye contact with each man in the room. He made each listener feel like his message was personal, as if he were directing his words to that man alone.

His name was Martin Richter, and he declared himself a candidate for Congress, running independently and unaffiliated with a major political party. He asserted that traditional party leadership lacked the foresight to endorse him, so he remained independent. The popinjay then dove into a forty minute speech that began with a testimonial to his love of America and its ideals then moved into a diatribe on the ills that ailed both Democrats and Republicans, what was wrong with big government and our craven society, and how the common man was ignored and abused by those in power. He spoke in even tones and concluded with the assurance that he was unlike other candidates. A vote for him would send a signal to Congressional leaders that the patriotic voters of Kansas would not stand for the Communistic policies, neglect, and abuse they had endured under President Roosevelt. Heads in the room bobbed up and down. It was clear that the men intended to back their candidate with their votes—and with their checkbooks.

Richter took questions and replied in sharp, terse phrases as if he'd anticipated the questions and rehearsed his answers. His broad smile stretched across his face and never extended to his eyes. His eyes remained cold and fixed. That smile disappeared when he spoke of President Roosevelt, who he referred to as "President Rosenstein." He called him a Communist, and heads bobbed again.

When he concluded, men rose from their chairs, stifled belches, and brought out their checkbooks. The cluster of roosters crowed and chattered, shook hands with one another, and slapped backs for several minutes before they filed out of the room. I remained seated in the corner until the FBI agents and their companion neared the door. When I stood up, Young acknowledged me with a nod.

"Stone, what brings you to this fancy gathering? Are you looking to invest your vast fortune in one of America's promising congressional candidates?"

"Maybe I am. Then again, maybe you brought me here. Maybe I'm tailing you now."

"Not a chance, gumshoe. You were here when we arrived. I spotted you in the corner when we crossed over the threshold."

I nodded at the third man.

"Who's your friend?"

Young glanced at the man.

"This is Aaron Bernstein, from Kansas City. He's doing field work for us."

I studied the well-dressed man. He looked too dapper and groomed to be a fed.

"Field work, huh? You don't strike me as the field work type, Bernstein," I said. "A guy in those threads wouldn't be working for what these chumps pay. You spend more on your cologne than these other two do on their shoes. You expect me to believe that line, Lennie? This guy doesn't work for you."

"Lay off, Stone," Young said. "You're not as smart as you think you are. There's a lot of things you don't know."

Bernstein wore the blue suit he'd worn at the Eaton, tailored to fit, set off by a flashy red tie trimmed in tan. His soft leather shoes cost more than a private eye or a government agent earned in a month. His pinkie finger sported a gold ring with a diamond setting, and he wore a gold Cartier watch on his left wrist. The man was moneyed, but not like the others I'd seen that evening. He belonged to a different ilk than the gentlemen who attended the soiree. He wouldn't fit in at a debutante's ball or a country club dining room. The jagged scar that crossed his chin wasn't the result of a razor nick, and fine clothes and expensive cologne didn't cover the man beneath. He looked expensive and smelled pretty, but he was tough and straight off the streets. He didn't belong to the FBI.

"Maybe I'm not smart," I said, "but I can spot a man who's connected. Is that it? Is the FBI hiring mobsters now, Lennie, gangsters on the payroll? Do these guys do your dirty work for you? How about it, Bernstein? Was it one of you who broke into my home?"

I fought to control my voice, but it was a losing battle. Bernstein raised his eyebrows and jutted his scarred chin.

"What're you talking about? Are you nuts, pal? Quit dishing the applesauce. Young, either you give this guy the bum's rush, or I will."

"That night at the Eaton. You followed me there," I said. "You sat at a table and read the paper, or you pretended to read the paper. You never turned the page. When I left, you made a phone call. Did you call my house and alert an accomplice to hightail it? Did you break into my home like these two broke into my office? You all have the same rotten M.O."

Bernstein feigned surprise.

"You're out of line, gumshoe," he said. "Yeah, I was at the Eaton. So, what? You were there, and I was there. You chatted with a dame. I saw you, and you saw me. I don't know from Adam about a break-in, and you don't know what you're talking about. You're Looney Tunes, straight outta the funny papers."

"Stone, he's right. You're out of line," Young said. "Stand down."

"Don't tell me to stand down. I'm not one of your field agents, or whatever you claim this bum to be. I don't know what you think I have, but whatever it is, I don't have it. Back off. Don't get in my way. Take your ball and roll it down the road. Stay out of my ball park."

I turned to Bernstein.

"That means you, too."

Bernstein looked like he'd enjoy taking a swing at me, and Young shook his head. No one spoke. I turned and walked out the door.

12

A call to a mobster and a
message from an old teammate.

Friday, April 29th

The next morning I placed a long distance telephone call. The operator took a name and a number, and I waited to be connected. Evan Vincent lived in Hot Springs, a resort town nestled in the rolling hills of western Arkansas. The town was a destination for tourists looking to bathe in its waters, swing to jazz music, guzzle hooch, and gamble on the ponies. The tourists brought money, and money brought the mob. The town developed a reputation as a place to have a good time while also earning a reputation as a hotbed of crime. Vincent fit right in.

He'd once plied his trade on the streets of New York City. Vincent, or Vinny to his pals, worked as a mobster and hired thug until he was invited to take a hike by the governor of New York. The governor had decided to run for president, and he figured that cleaning up crime in the country's largest city would garner publicity and votes. He went to work to rid the Big Apple of its seedier elements. Vinny and others like him were urged to skedaddle, the implication being either leave on a train or wind up in a box. Vinny headed south.

The governor's campaign got results. He won the election in a landslide. Governor Roosevelt became President Roosevelt, and FDR took up residence in a big, white house in Washington, D.C.

Vinny landed in Hot Springs. The address changed, but the new town and new digs didn't alter Vinny the man. He wasn't cut out to sell Bibles or clerk in a haberdashery, and once he settled in he resumed his former career in crime.

Our paths crossed when I visited the resort town on an earlier case. I happened to be present in a popular watering hole the night an angry gunman accosted Vinny. The former nemesis from New York City was intent on plugging holes in Evan Vincent. I subdued the man before he pulled the trigger, and Vinny's life was spared. He was grateful to me for saving his life, and the two of us formed a mutual admiration for each other, a tenuous friendship of sorts.

The operator made the connection, and a feminine voice came on the line.

"Hello? This is Mr. Vincent's answering service. Mr. Vincent is unavailable at this time, but I can take a message. May I ask who is calling?"

I gave the lady my name, and I left a message for Vinny outlining what I needed.

"Thank you, Mr. Stone. Mr. Vincent is away at the moment, but he checks his messages regularly. I'll give him your message the moment he calls in. What is your telephone number, please?"

Vincent had my number, but I repeated it for the woman, and she assured me again that she'd pass the message on to him. I hung up the telephone and reached for the newspaper. I scanned the headlines and turned to the sports page when Agnes knocked and came into my office.

"I took a telephone call from a man who'd like to see you this afternoon. He said he'd be here by five o'clock, but he wanted to make sure you'd be in the office. I told him you would be. Is that okay? He said you knew each other years ago. His name is Sam Orsulak."

I let out a low whistle.

"Sam Orsulak," I said. "Now there's a name I haven't spoken in a long time. I wonder what Sam Orsulak wants. Sure, I'll be here. Thanks, Agnes."

Years had passed since I last saw Sam Orsulak. Maybe not enough years. We hadn't parted on the best of terms. We once played baseball together, the two of us along with Cocky Wright and a fluid roster of other players who came and went. We played on the same team for several summers until that one day long ago in a ball yard on the edge of El Dorado. On a Sunday afternoon, our team of farm boys challenged a team made up of oilfield roughnecks. Folks for miles around came to watch. The men parked their jalopies along the boundaries of the field, the vehicles forming a fence of sorts. Women spread blankets on the grass and unpacked picnic baskets laden with fried chicken, ears of corn, apple pies, and watermelons. Children ran around and played and shrieked and had a grand time. Men clustered in a copse of cottonwood trees and sipped beer in the shade. They also placed bets on the outcome of the game.

The game meant little to the world and everything to the community. Pride and bragging rights were on the line, and hefty wads of cash backed up the braggadocio. Both teams played hard, and the lead went back and forth. The summer sun bore down on the ball field as well as the players and fans. Players guzzled long swallows of water between innings and wiped sweat from their brows with their shirttails. Fans grew animated and tense, long on bravado and short of temper.

Our farm boys had the lead, but the roughnecks had the tying runner on third base when their man at the plate hit a towering pop fly over our shortstop. All eyes were on the ball. It rose high in the air, but it figured to be a sure out until one of the fans butted in. From my position in centerfield, I heard a voice yell from the sidelines, "Twenty bucks if you let it drop!"

What happened in the next couple of seconds changed lives. Our shortstop glanced toward the sidelines and took a step back.

He moved away from the ball. Cocky played second base, but he had moved over from his position toward the ball to back up the play. When our shortstop moved away, Cocky dove forward and skidded on his chest in the base path. The ball landed in his glove. In a single motion, he slid in the dirt, caught the ball, and sprang to his feet. He never slowed down. He yelled timeout to the umpire and ran toward the sidelines. He faced the crowd and addressed them in a firm voice.

"Which one yelled?" he said.

No one spoke, but fans stepped back and parted and left one soul standing alone. Cocky stuck his nose in the man's face.

"Pay him," he said.

The man stuttered and protested.

"But you caught the ball!" the man said.

He backed up a step, and Cocky stayed with him, nose to nose. Cocky didn't budge. Even from the outfield I could see the muscles in Cocky's jaw clinch. The man glanced to his left and to his right looking for support. He found none. Cocky didn't blink. The man reached into his pocket and fumbled out a twenty dollar bill. Cocky snatched the bill from his hand and turned on his heel. Everyone watched him as he strode back onto the field. This time he faced our shortstop, nose to nose, and stuffed the twenty dollar bill into the guy's shirt pocket.

"Get off the field," he said. "You're finished here. Find another team."

The guy left. All of that took place when we were young men. Years passed. I never saw or heard from that man again, not until that day. That day he called my office. Sam Orsulak called and left a message saying he wanted to see me. Why? What could Sam Orsulak want with me all these years later, and why was I willing to meet with a has-been ballplayer who sold out his team for a twenty dollar bill?

♦ ♦ ♦

13
Strange bedfellows.

Friday, April 29th

Noon arrived, and I told Agnes I'd hold down the fort while she went to lunch. I wanted to be at my desk when Vinny returned my telephone call. I had the newspaper in one hand and a cup of coffee in the other when Agnes came back twenty minutes later. She unloaded a brown paper sack on my desk.

I grinned and savored the smells. Agnes brought NuWay hamburger sandwiches wrapped in grease-stained paper along with sliced dill pickles and the spicy mustard she knew I favored. She poured fresh coffee for both of us and took a seat across the desk from me. We dug in. Loose meat from the burgers dribbled onto our paper napkins. Agnes nibbled at a pickle and added a slice or two atop her sandwich. I wiped a dollop of mustard from the corner of my mouth. The food hit the spot.

"This is swell, really good," I said. "I didn't even know I was hungry. How do you always know what I need?"

She rolled her eyes.

"You're a man, aren't you? Men are predictable, all men including you."

She chewed slowly and looked wistful.

"I suppose I am predictable," I said. "Every man likes to pretend he has a poker face—that he's good at the game and difficult to read—but few are. You look pensive, kiddo. What's on your mind?"

"Oh, nothing really."

"You don't own the greatest poker face yourself, you know."

She chewed slowly before she spoke.

"Do you ever wish for more?" she said.

"More?"

"Yeah, you know. More than what you've got."

"More money? A better job?"

"No, that's not it. More out of life, I guess. I don't know."

I thought that over. Agnes once pined for a career on Broadway or at least on a stage in Kansas City, something more than Wichita had to offer.

"I like what I do," I said. "I suppose I had bigger dreams when I was younger, but we reach an age, and we are who we are. No one will ever read about me in the history books, but I like being a private eye. You once dreamed of dancing in the footlights as I recall. You hoped to hoof it didn't you? And sing? Maybe whisper into the microphone, croon slow tunes in a sultry saloon? Still have those dreams?"

"Huh. Are you kidding? Those dreams shriveled as my hips widened."

I raised an eyebrow.

"Well, widened just a bit," she said. "I dream those dreams from time to time, sure, but it isn't healthy to dwell on things we can't change. You enjoy being a detective, but that wasn't always your plan in life was it? How about when you were a boy? What ran through your mind when you were a schoolboy, when you were bored with the teacher and stared out the window during class?"

She took a bite of sandwich.

"That's easy. I was going to play centerfield for the New York Yankees, shag fly balls in the Bronx. The bums turned me down, though. They gave the job to Joe DiMaggio and paid him twenty-five grand to do it. It's their loss. I'd have taken the job for a fraction of that."

"The Yankees? I thought all you men hated the Yankees."

"Not all of us. For some of us it's a love-hate relationship. The Yankees are the best team in baseball, and the classiest. Those pinstripe uniforms are the snappiest in the game, hands down. They ink good players, too, the best. They win more games than other teams. Even when they don't, they're the team to beat. Everybody loves a winner, and everybody loves it when a winner get his nose bloodied. Love them. Hate them. It's complicated."

"Why centerfield?"

I shrugged. "It's the way I'm built, I guess. It suits me. Centerfield is freedom, room to roam. No one in baseball covers more ground than the centerfielder."

"Room to roam. That does sound like you."

The telephone rang. I answered it, and Evan Vincent was on the line.

"Vinny, thanks for returning my call," I said.

Agnes picked up the remains of her lunch, and I mouthed a thank you to her before she moved to her desk in the outer office.

"Always good to hear from my favorite gumshoe," he said. "It's been too long. Don't be a stranger. Why don't you hop into that roadster of yours and drive down for a few days? Take in the waters and visit one of my clubs. We can play the ponies in the afternoon."

"I'm tempted, Vinny, but I've got something going right now, and I need to see it through."

"Okay, see it through, then come on down."

"I'll take you up on the waters and the club scene," I said, "but only a fool would play the ponies against Evan Vincent in Hot Springs."

Vincent laughed and said, "I'll let you win a race or two."

"I left a message when I called," I said. "I'm trying to get a line on a guy named Aaron Bernstein, out of Kansas City. Do you know anything?"

"Yeah, I got your message. I never heard of the guy, but I made a call to KC. What made you think Bernstein was connected?"

"He claims to be with the FBI, and they back him up," I said, "but nothing about the guy fits. He's a dapper dresser, wears tailored threads and flashy gewgaws. The feds say he's doing field work for them, but I don't buy that story either. He doesn't fit the profile of a G-man. He looks connected, but that doesn't fit if he's arm-in-arm with the feds. I wondered if you knew anything about him."

"Well, your instincts were right," Vincent said. "The guy is connected. Aaron Bernstein is a lieutenant in the Jewish mob out of Kansas City. Gambles, runs a numbers racket, sports betting. I've never met him, but I rubbed elbows with some of his associates in the city—New York City, that is."

"So, Aaron Bernstein, is a mobster, and he's working with the FBI," I said. "What's the connection?"

He laughed and said, "Strange bedfellows."

Then his tone grew serious.

"Maybe not so strange at that," he said.

"What do you mean?" I said.

"After I called Kansas City, I made another telephone call to New York City. What I got was an earful of rumor. There's always rumors in this business, but the guy I spoke to is on the money more often than not. He tells me that the government is investigating foreign agents sneaking into the country, coming through ports of entry in the northeast. The feds want to put a halt to it. They're looking, but they're coming up empty. They're scared, and they're helpless. So guess who they turn to for help? If you wanted the inside dope on smuggling, maybe sabotage, who would you turn to?"

"I'd turn to the guys who wrote the book on smuggling and sabotage," I said, "the mob."

"Like I said, this is all just rumor," Vinny said, "but the word on the street is the fed contacted the head of the Jewish mob for help, and they've also called on an Italian mobster who's doing time in the pen. They moved him to a new location closer to the city, more convenient. No names or details, pal, just rumors. Something to keep in mind."

"Thanks, Vinny. I owe you one."

"Anytime. Come and see me. We'll play the ponies, and you'll win the first race. I guarantee it."

I listened to his laugh as I cradled the receiver. The Jewish mob and the FBI were working together. Vinny was right. They were strange bedfellows indeed.

14

A meeting and a bribe.

Friday, April 29th

The mountain of flesh that filled the doorway was no one I recognized. Agnes ushered the man into my office and said she'd go on home unless I needed her to stay. The hands on the Seth Thomas Banjo clock approached five o'clock. I told Agnes to call it a day. She left with a wave, and the man walked in and stuck out a paw.

"How are you, Pete? It's been a long time."

I recognized the voice and shook the man's hand.

"Sam? Sam Orsulak?"

"I've put on a little weight," he said.

I motioned to a chair, and he lowered himself onto the seat. Both he and the chair groaned. The big man wore denim overalls and a blue chambray shirt with a patch stitched onto the sleeve that read Boeing alongside the company logo. His salt and pepper hair was clipped short to the scalp. A bit of fuzz on one of his chins pretended to be a goatee. I moved to my chair behind the desk.

"Like you said, it's been a long time," I said. "You're working for Boeing, huh? That's terrific. They're a good company. Been there long?"

"Almost twelve years. I'm an inspector, recent promotion. I check the welds, the seams, the nuts and bolts, that sort of thing. I decide when a plane is ready to fly. Nothing goes up until I do my job."

Sam made himself sound important, but his job was one of hundreds at a company that size. Nothing got off the ground at Boeing until a welder formed those seams and a mechanic screwed the nuts and bolts together. An airplane didn't fly until a lot of good people did their jobs. That's the thought that came to my mind, but I didn't mention it.

"There's a nice future in aviation, especially now during this Depression," I said. "It's a growing industry, and I've heard good things about Boeing. In fact, I was just talking about your company with a fellow I know at Stearman. You must know Stearman. It's soon to become a part of Boeing, you know. Cocky Wright worked there. Remember Cocky? He died recently."

He nodded.

"I heard about that, yes. Terrible accident."

"It was terrible, yes. Did you cross paths with Cocky? Maybe speak to him after he went to work at Stearman?"

"No, I never spoke to him. I didn't know Cocky worked at Stearman until I heard about the accident. The Boeing factory is down the road, further south on Oliver. I drive by Stearman every day, but I've never stopped."

I raised an eyebrow. Orsulak was lying. I had seen him at Stearman on two occasions, first when he inspected the cockpit of a trainer plane and again when he drove away in his car. I hadn't recognized him either time, but the man in my office was the man I'd seen at Stearman. Like I told Agnes, I owned a lousy poker face. A good player would have noticed my expression, but it slipped by Orsulak, and he continued talking.

"I might've stopped to say hello to Cocky if I'd known he was there. You know, try to heal old wounds. I guess it's too late for that now."

"Yeah, too late. So, what brings Sam Orsulak to see Pete Stone? Are you looking up an old acquaintance or do you need the services of a gumshoe?"

"Neither. Maybe both. I wasn't sure you'd see me after all this time. After that game, you remember the one, lots of teammates fell away from me. Actually, all of them fell away. No one spoke to me after that day."

His tone was defensive and unapologetic. I shrugged.

"That was a tough day for all of us," I said. "We played to win. We didn't have much back then, but we had our pride. Winning meant something. We didn't throw games."

"Times were tough," he said. "That money meant a lot to me."

"Times were tough for all of us," I said and leaned back in my chair. "Let's begin this conversation again. How about a cup of coffee?"

He nodded, so I went to the outer office and returned with two cups of coffee. Sam held an unlit cigarette, so I lit his and one for myself. I returned to my chair. Neither of us spoke for a minute or so. We smoked and drank coffee until I broke the silence.

"That was a lifetime ago," I said. "Let's move ahead. You didn't come here to reminisce. What's on your mind?"

"I didn't come here on my own. Someone sent me to see you. Let's say he strongly urged me to see you."

"Who strongly urged you to see me?"

"I can't tell you his name, but you'll know soon enough. If you play along, that is."

"What do you mean if I play along? What is this, Orsulak? Shoot straight and make sense. Give me the dope and can the secrecy. Why are you here? Why is this guy interested in a private dick like me? Why not come to me himself? My door is open."

"Let me finish," he said. "The man who sent me wants to meet with you but not here. He has his reasons. He instructed me to take you to him. In fact, he's waiting for you now. If you agree, I'm supposed to drive you there."

"Drive me? I can drive myself. What are you involved in?"

He puffed his cigarette and swallowed his coffee before he spoke.

"Somebody connected the dots between us, between you and Cocky Wright and me. They found out that we once played ball together. That's why he sent me. I guess he figured we were old friends. I'm as surprised about it as you are, but the man in question wants to talk to you, and my orders are to deliver you to him. Just you and me, although Cocky's name may come up. "

He mentioned Cocky again. I tossed my cigarette butt into the ashtray, placed both of my palms on the desk, and leaned forward.

"Sam, tell me right now on the square. Did you or anyone else you know have anything to do with Cocky's death?"

"Easy, Pete," he said. "That was an accident. I had nothing to do with Cocky's death. I'm a messenger and a delivery boy. Somebody wants to talk to you. Maybe a wealthy eccentric wants to hire you. You could stand to profit. I'm the lackey doing his bidding. I was given a time and a place. The time is now, and the place isn't far."

"What makes you think the man is wealthy?"

Sam kept the man's address to himself, but he described a neighborhood in the College Hill district, classy and highbrow. A house in that area belonged to Henry Allen, a former governor of our state. Allen had hired the well-known architect, Frank Lloyd Wright, to design and build his sprawling mansion. Every citizen in Wichita knew of the residence. The homes nearby were stunning, too. Orsulak's assumption was correct. The man who wanted to see me had to be well-heeled. His level of eccentricity remained to be determined.

"I'll meet with your mystery moneybags," I said, "but I can drive myself. I know the neighborhood. Give me an address. I'll show up."

"No can do, pal. My instructions are specific. I'm to drive you to his doorstep and wait for you there. Then I'll drive you back here. Otherwise I don't get my dough."

It was always about the money, I thought to myself. Orsulak

rose from his chair and groaned, but in my imagination the chair sighed in relief. We left the office together.

The route we traveled took us from my office downtown to the north and east toward College Hill. At First and Roosevelt we turned north and passed by the Allen mansion, a prairie style home in rust colored brick with a red tile roof. At Second Street we turned a corner, and in another block Orsulak slowed his vehicle. Towering oak trees cast long shadows over a white-columned house. The neighborhood was in Wichita, but the landscape conjured images of Twelve Oaks, the Ashley Wilkes plantation in Georgia that Margaret Mitchell described in *Gone with the Wind,* her novel of the Civil War. A driveway lined with trimmed shrubs and flowerbeds wound through the manicured lawn.

Orsulak maneuvered the car, the steering wheel rubbing against folds of denim covered flesh. He turned the wheel hand over hand onto the driveway and guided the vehicle along the circuitous path. He pulled up in front of a half-moon porch and braked to a stop. I breathed out a low whistle.

"The guy with the key to this palace swims in the deep end of the pool," I said. "Who is he and how did you come to meet him?"

Sam shook his head.

"You ask too many questions. You'll find out soon enough. I'll be right here when you're finished."

"They don't have an entrance for the delivery boy?" I said. "The guy with the deed to this place must've figured a detective could find it on his own, but he sends you to taxi me and then leaves you in the driveway. That's rude."

"I'm just following orders. Get out. No, wait a minute. I'm supposed to frisk you first. Orders."

I raised my eyebrows.

"Forget the frisk. I'm not carrying a gun."

Sam stared at me. I shook my head and unbuttoned my coat. He didn't frisk me, but his pudgy fingers held my coat open so he could inspect me. He looked to the left and to the right.

"Okay," he said. "Get out and ring the bell."

I exited the car onto the pebbled walkway and climbed three steps to the porch landing. I pushed the button, and soft chimes announced my arrival. A moment later one of the double doors opened. A gray-haired butler in a black tuxedo greeted me with a slight bow and ushered me in.

"You are expected, Mr. Stone. This way, please. May I take your hat?"

I handed it over and followed the butler through a great room lit by chandeliers. Framed artwork covered the walls. A spiral staircase led to an upper floor, and at the top of the winding stairs I glimpsed the hem of a satin housecoat above a dainty ankle. The housecoat and the ankle disappeared through a doorway, and the door snicked shut. The butler led me into a study.

"The master of the house sends his apologies," he said. "He was unavoidably detained, but he'll arrive momentarily. May I get you a drink while you wait?"

"No, thanks. Say, who is the master of the house, anyway?"

"As I say, he'll be right along. You may wait here."

He bowed his head and left me in the study. The room was furnished in French provincial décor with a desk, sofa, and wingback chairs. A Persian rug covered the floor. An unlit fireplace occupied one wall, and the other walls were lined with bookshelves and art. Leather-bound books appeared organized, dust free, and unread. I moved toward a framed painting on the wall behind the desk.

The painting portrayed an adolescent girl with long, red curls who wore a white dress and a wide-brimmed straw hat. I leaned in closer, mesmerized by the girl's clear, blue eyes. I glanced at the artist's signature and saw a name I recognized, Robert Henri. I had once visited Henri's boyhood hometown in Cozad, Nebraska.

His father founded the town and christened it with the family name. Henri was raised in Cozad, but when his father shot a man over a land dispute, the family departed and never returned. Henri adopted a new last name, a variant of his middle name, Henry, but he eschewed the French pronunciation. The artist pronounced his name as Hen Rye. He studied painting and built a reputation in the art community. His talent was highly regarded, and his paintings had increased in value since his death in the previous decade. The painting held my attention. The model's eyes haunted me, as if I'd seen those eyes before.

A door stood ajar at the end of the study. From the doorway, I scanned the contents of the adjoining room, a single bed, a lamp and radio on a nightstand, along with a French provincial chair with a pair of trousers draped across the back. I glanced over my shoulder. I was alone. I couldn't resist. I entered the room and opened a door to a walk-in closet that held an array of suits, trousers, sports coats, and at least a dozen pairs of shoes. I'd shopped in stores that offered slighter inventories. I counted thirty-seven sports coats before a loud "ahem" interrupted me. The butler stood outside the closet and glared.

"My mistake," I said. "I must've taken a wrong turn. I was looking for the gent's."

"The gentleman's room is outside and down the hall," the butler said in an icy tone. "The master of the house has arrived."

We moved into the hallway, and the butler gestured toward a closed door. He waited with his hands behind his back while I went into the bathroom. After a moment, I flushed the toilet and ran water in the sink. The butler held his glare when I returned to the hallway.

"Thank you," I said. "Much better."

"This way," he said.

We went into a parlor, also furnished in French provincial style. People of a high class didn't purchase furniture piece by piece or shop for bargains like a seedy private detective might. People of that class selected a décor, called on a fine retailer, and purchased furniture by the roomful. In the parlor, a tall gentlemen stood with his back to me and mixed drinks atop a sideboard.

"Mr. Stone," the butler announced.

"Thank you, Maynard," the tall man said, and Maynard the butler backed out of the room. The tall man finished his task and turned toward me holding a pair of martinis garnished with olives. He extended one in my direction. I took it without looking at it. My eyes never left his.

"Well, if it isn't Mr. Martin Richter," I said, "or should I say Congressman Richter?"

"Martin is fine. It's premature to call me Congressman, but I appreciate the gesture. I trust the voters will grant me the honor of that title in November. And you are Pete Stone, private detective. I recognize you. You attended my meeting last night at the Hotel Lassen, and now here you are. What did you think of our get-together?"

"Yes, I attended. I apologize for not donating to your campaign. I must have left my checkbook in my other trousers."

The corners of his mouth curled into a grin, but that grin did not extend to his eyes. His eyes were cold and without expression. A thought of the painting in the study came to mind, and I recalled where I'd seen the girl's blue eyes. They belonged to the auburn-haired dame that exited Richter's cab that day at the Forum. His wife, I suspected. The girl in the painting was a younger version of the woman I'd seen that day. The girl had grown into a woman, but the years hadn't tempered those ice-blue eyes.

"Don't fret over your checkbook, Mr. Stone. In fact, that's the reason I asked you to be here. I'd like to add a little money to your bank account. I'd like to hire you, if you're willing to play ball, that is. How's your martini?"

I sipped my drink.

"Best martini I've ever tasted," I said, and it was the truth.

"It's made with Boodles gin," he said. "A little hard to come by these days, but one manages."

I scanned the décor and spotted more artwork including another painting by Henri. This one depicted a young boy with pursed lips and wide blue eyes that bore into the viewer's soul. A bronze statue of a cowboy on a rearing horse seemed out of place atop the provincial end table, but smart money would wager the sculpture was crafted by Frederic Remington.

"It looks as though you mange quite well. What could a gumshoe like me do for a man like you?"

"Don't be so modest, Mr. Stone. It doesn't become you."

He gestured toward a pair of chairs. We sat down, and it came to me, the reason why I was summoned and delivered to this place. Richter wanted me in his parlor and not in my office so he could gain home field advantage, an old trick. The French décor, the artwork, the chandeliers, the Boodles, and all the rest were props in a play, a king's method of exhibiting control and gaining power over his pawn.

"I'm looking for something you can deliver," he said, "something valuable to me. The most valuable commodity to a man in my profession is information. You are the link to information I need. Maybe you have it or maybe you don't. If you don't, you are searching for it, too. In either case, I wish to buy that information, and I'm willing to pay you handsomely for it."

"Exactly what is it you're after, Richter?" I said. "You presume I have something or I'm hot on its trail. What is it I have?"

He sipped his martini and lowered his glass. His grin faded, and his charm disappeared. He wore an expression that said he'd discovered something disgusting on the sole of his shoe.

"Stop trying to be coy, Stone. Federal agents have been in contact with you. I know that, and I know that they're after information, too. Before you decide to work with them, you should consider your own welfare. The feds won't pay you what I'm willing to pay. The information in question is sensitive to a man in my position. I want it before they get it."

He looked me in the eyes and sipped his Boodles.

"Maybe you're on the level," he said. "Maybe you don't have what I'm after, not yet, anyway. If not, I'm willing to bet you will have it. Until then, there's no reason to discuss what it is or bring it into the open. When you find it, you'll know."

"You're speaking in riddles," I said. "You want information, and you're willing to pay for it, but you won't tell me what that information is. Does this have anything to do with my friend, Cocky Wright?"

Richter furrowed his brow.

"I didn't know your friend," he said. "I never met him, but he stole something that didn't belong to him. That I know. He didn't steal it from me, but it concerns me nevertheless."

"If he didn't steal it from you, who did he steal it from? Pettigrew?"

He flinched at the mention of Pettigrew's name.

"Maybe Wright left something with you. I'm asking. Did he leave anything with you?"

"If he had left anything with me, information or anything else of value for that matter, I wouldn't discuss it with you. And if I discover anything that suggests his death wasn't an accident, anything that points to your involvement in his death, you won't have a chance to ask questions. You'll be staring down the barrel of a heater."

"Easy, Stone. Okay, we're both looking for information. Our interests are not mutually exclusive. I'd still like to hire you."

Richter removed an envelope from his breast pocket. He took out a bill and flashed a portrait of Grover Cleveland. It was on a thousand dollar bill.

"There are four more of these inside this envelope," he said. "They are all yours, five thousand dollars, paid in advance for any information you locate. All you have to do is bring it to me and not the FBI."

He tossed the envelope onto a table next to my chair.

"What happens if I don't find what you're after?" I said. "What happens if there is no information?"

"Then you keep the money. I'm not worried. If there is anything to be found, you'll find it. Your methods may be unorthodox, but I understand you always find what you look for. I'm not interested in how you do your job. I just want what you find."

"Five thousand dollars for something I don't even have," I said. "Whatever it is, it must be valuable. A guy who drinks pricey gin and hangs fine art on the walls didn't come into dough by spending it foolishly."

"Never mind how I got my money. Do we have an agreement or not?"

I shook my head.

"No dice," I said. "I don't know what you're after, but if you're willing to lay five G's on the line, it's got to be worth more than that."

"Don't be a fool," he said. "That's more money than a chump like you makes in a year. I didn't always have wealth, you know. I was raised on beans and cornbread."

I thought about that painting of the young girl with red hair and blue eyes. It took some serious cash to commission Henri to do that portrait. The woman's parents probably paid the artist. Richter might have married into his cozy berth. I didn't care. I stood up and put my empty glass on the sideboard.

"Thanks for the Boodles," I said.

"You'll come around," he said and rose from his chair. "Take this for your trouble."

He stuffed a bill into the breast pocket of my coat.

"We're not so different," he said. "I get what I go after, too. The money in that envelope is yours when you change your mind."

I didn't look at the bill in my pocket or the envelope on the table, and I didn't shake Richter's hand when I left the parlor. I walked out of the room and headed to the front door. The butler had my hat in his hand.

"Thank you, Maynard," I said.

Maynard offered me the hat with one hand and served up a glare with both eyes. Why shouldn't he? They all had cold eyes in that place. Cold eyes furnished the joint. The door closed behind me. I took in a deep breath of fresh air, stepped off the porch, and climbed into the car that waited for me, idling in the driveway.

15
A lady whose name meant sorrows.

Saturday, April 30th

The lady stood on the pebbled walkway and waited for the taxicab to roll to a stop. Auburn curls fell to her shoulders. A blue dress with white polka dots hugged her slender frame and flared below the knees. A blue cloche rested over her curls, and a matching silk scarf was draped loosely around her neck. Her eyes weren't visible from a distance, but I knew they matched her blue outfit. The cabbie hopped out of his vehicle and held open the rear door for the lady. She placed one hand on the door, and the nails on her delicate fingers glistened scarlet in the sunlight. The red nails matched her lipstick.

I watched her from my position down the street. I'd been sitting in my car for a couple of hours. When her husband left the house and drove off in a car, I thought I'd ring the bell and visit with the lady of the house—alone. I never got the chance. The cab arrived shortly after the car departed.

When the cab rolled out of the driveway, I started my roadster and tailed it. The cab went west and dropped south headed toward downtown. Traffic picked up as we neared the center of the city, but the cabdriver was experienced. He navigated around vehicles and through traffic signals with minimum delay and came to a halt in the two hundred block of South Broadway, in front of the Allis Hotel. The lady settled with the driver and entered the hotel. I parked my roadster alongside the curb, doffed my fedora to the doorman at the entrance, and followed her into the lobby.

The Allis was a grand hotel, seventeen stories of Art Deco design and the tallest building in the state. Celebrities, politicians, high rollers with deep pockets, and mucky-mucks traveling on the other guy's nickel all signed the register at the Allis. I once spotted Jimmy Durante exiting the hotel wearing a big grin beneath his trademark schnoz. Adoring fans rushed him and fell in his wake. Durante mugged for his fans and followed that nose out the door and onto the sidewalk. He stopped there to accommodate autograph seekers before disappearing into a waiting limousine.

The lady I followed strolled through the lobby with an elegance and grace that turned heads, one high-heeled shoe falling softly in front of the other. She disappeared into the hotel beauty shop. I glanced at my watch and stepped into the Kit Kat coffee shop to wait. I took a seat that faced the lobby and the beauty shop and ordered a cup of coffee. The coffee and the hotel ambience were welcome. I'd wait to see her and speak to her. I wanted to be alone with her, without her husband's knowledge and free from the prying eyes and ears of a butler.

An hour later, almost to the minute, the lady exited the salon. She stopped in the lobby and glanced at her watch. Her styled auburn curls fell to her shoulders, and the nails on her fingers shone glossy and red. She looked fresh, radiant, and beautiful— exactly like she looked before she walked into the salon. I'd already settled my tab with the waitress, so I left the coffee shop. I intended to catch the lady before she hailed a cab.

She moved toward the concierge's desk, but paused before reaching it. She turned to her right and entered the hotel dining room. I waited in the lobby for several minutes and gave her time to get seated, then I went into the dining room myself. The maître d' offered to seat me, but I shook my head and nodded toward the lady. She sat alone in a booth in a dimly lit corner at the rear of the restaurant. A waiter moved away from her table. She sipped amber liquid from a stemmed cocktail glass. Skewered cherries on a swizzle stick lay on a saucer next to an ashtray that held a smoldering cigarette. The Allis didn't serve liquor to its patrons, not to my knowledge, anyway. The lady had class, and she had pull. I walked over to the booth with my hat in my hand and watched her crush out the cigarette.

"Mind if I join you?" I said.

She looked up and raised her eyebrows. She didn't speak. She motioned to the seat across the table. I took it.

"Thank you," I said.

The waiter appeared at my elbow.

"The lady will have another, Manhattan is it?" I said.

The waiter nodded.

"And for the gentleman?"

"I'll have what the lady is having. Except, hold the vermouth. Come to think of it, hold the bitters, too. And lose the cherries."

The waiter rolled his eyes.

"Perhaps the gentleman would care for a glass of bourbon?"

"On the rocks," I said.

The waiter nodded and left. I lit a cigarette and studied the lady. The lady sipped her Manhattan and studied me.

"Frankly, I'm surprised," I said. "You allowed a strange man to sit down with you. I'm pleased, you understand, but surprised. Why did you do that?"

She lifted the swizzle stick and removed a single cherry with her ruby lips. She rolled the cherry into her mouth, offered an unblinking stare with those ice blue eyes, and chewed slowly. Then she raised her cocktail, sipped the amber liquid, and lowered the empty glass.

"You came to my home last evening. You spoke with my husband. It didn't go well. On a prior occasion you politely stepped aside and allowed me to enter a doorway at the Forum. You are a private detective, and your name is Pete Stone. I'd hardly call you a strange man."

The waiter arrived with our drinks and retreated with a slight bow.

"I'm impressed," I said. "You have an eye for detail."

"Don't be. I find none of that in the least bit interesting. However, my husband offered you a great deal of money to do some work for him, and you refused to take it. That does intrigue me."

"What if I said I recently came into a pile of dough and decided I didn't have to work for a while?"

"Ha."

"What if I said the job sounds too dangerous and I fear for my life?"

"Ha."

"What if I said I don't like your husband and I want nothing to do with him or his money?"

"That sounds more like it."

She removed another cigarette from her purse, and I held a flame to it.

"You have me at a disadvantage, Mrs. Richter. You know something about me, but I know nothing about you. Shall I call you missus or do you have a first name?"

She blew a puff of smoke toward the ceiling.

"It's Delores."

"Delores. That's a lovely name."

"It means sorrows. It suits me."

"Now it's my turn to say ha. You're a beautiful woman, a woman of means. You're married to an up-and-coming political figure, a man who has the ear of well-heeled community leaders. You live in a lavish home tricked with fine art and expensive furnishings, and as an added bonus you're spending a quiet afternoon in an elegant establishment with a dazzling detective. Sounds pretty good to me. Why the sorrows?"

"You should meet my father. You two would get along famously. Why are you following me? You met my husband and you didn't like him, not that I blame you, so what made you follow me here?"

I talked, and she listened. I told her about Cocky, how he died and my doubt that the crash was an accident. I wondered what he had that interested her husband, and I wondered if her husband was involved in his death. She listened without interruption, then she crushed out her cigarette and leaned back in the booth.

"I'm sorry your friend died," she said, "but my husband had nothing to do with it. My husband wouldn't be involved in anything like that."

"He wouldn't be involved in murder?"

"He wouldn't be involved in people. It's not that he doesn't care about them. He's simply unaware they exist, as people, that is. To him people are either tools or obstacles. They are to be used to get what he wants or they are to be leapt over when they get in the way, nothing more. I apologize for being so blunt, but your friend the aircraft mechanic would hold no interest for my husband."

"You're wrong," I said. "Your husband offered me five grand to buy information I don't even have. He thinks my friend had it and passed it on to me. I don't have it, and I don't know what that information is. Five grand spells interest to me."

She finished her second Manhattan, and I pointed to her empty glass. She shook her head. The waiter had approached the booth, but when he saw her decline my offer, he retreated.

"You're right," she said. "Information might interest my husband. Still, he'd never be involved in murder, not that he isn't capable. He wouldn't have to be involved. He'd order an underling to get what he wanted. He'd give no thought as to how the underling did his bidding."

"Who would that underling be?" I said.

"It could be anybody. An underling is whoever my husband talks to."

"You don't like your husband much, do you? It's none of my business, but you have beauty, and you talk like you have brains. If your husband drives you to retreat to the shadows to nurse a cocktail, why are you with him? Is it the money?"

She chuckled.

"Men. You're all so smart. Are you married?"

"No," I said.

"But there's a woman?"

"Yes."

She considered that.

"No, it isn't money that keeps my marriage alive, not in the way you think it does, anyway. My father warned me against marrying Martin. He told me I'd be sorry, but I was headstrong and independent, just like the man who raised me. Maybe my father looked at Martin and saw himself. My father gave me an ultimatum—give up Martin or else. I considered my options and chose or else."

She reached for another cigarette. I lit it and another cigarette for myself. The maître d' seated a man and a woman at a table across the floor, but the restaurant remained hushed.

"I was charmed by the man," she said. "He spun a web of lies, but his lies didn't matter. I listened and believed because I wanted to believe. Martin still spins webs and tells lies. That's who he is, but now he casts his spell over others. A wide audience believes what he says. He understands people better than they do themselves. People don't want to hear the truth. People want to hear what they want to hear. They'll listen to almost anything, if it's what they want to hear. They'll embrace any idea if it's repeated loudly enough and often enough. Martin knows this. People want to believe him, and so they do. My father recognized him for what he is, a liar and a charlatan. It's not money that keeps me tied to Martin Richter. It's pride. If I left him, I'd have to face my father and admit I was wrong. I couldn't do that."

"I wear the chain I forged in life," I said.

"Jacob Marley's ghost," she said. "Just so you understand, the money isn't Martin's. It's mine."

I raised my eyebrows.

"Surprised?" she said. "Surprised that a woman like me can be well-heeled, as you say? Well, it's true. I was raised in Kansas City. My father inherited a small fortune. He turned it into a large fortune. Part of that inheritance came to me in a trust. I wanted to believe that Martin saw me and wanted me and not my money. I hoped he saw an attractive and desirable woman. He didn't. He told me I was attractive and desirable, but those were just words. I believed him because I wanted to believe him. He lied to me. Now, I'm married to him, but I sleep alone. All he saw in me was a meal ticket."

I recalled something Richter had told me, "I didn't always have wealth, you know. I grew up on beans and cornbread."

"I thought he loved me," she said. "It turns out he loved my money more."

There was nothing left to discuss. I stared into those blue eyes and marveled at the depth of beauty and sadness I saw there. She declined my offer to drive her home. I stood up and dropped some bills onto the table and said goodbye. I left Delores Richter sitting in the shadows, a beautiful, rich, and lonely woman whose name meant sorrows.

16
My Melancholy Baby.

Saturday, April 30th & Sunday, May 1st

The juke joint jumped. I tapped my toes to notes and tunes, but my mind drifted. Failed elevators on the Stearman trainer caused the crash that killed Cocky. The authorities deemed the crash an accident. I didn't buy it. If it was an accident, why not bury the dead and move on? Cocky's name kept popping up. Cocky had something that lots of people wanted. The FBI, aircraft employees, and a wannabe Congressman married to a sad, beautiful wife wanted something Cocky had. Orsulak was connected to Richter. How did he fit in? He lied to me when he said he hadn't visited Stearman. There was also the out of town stranger who had underestimated Sundown, a fatal last mistake. He threatened her with a pistol, and she blew him away with a shotgun. The hogs feasted on his remains. Would someone else come for Sundown? I considered the key Sundown had given me and the empty envelope with my name printed on the front. How did it all add up?

"Earth to Pete Stone. Come in Pete Stone."

The voice belonged to Lucille.

"Oh, sorry," I said.

"Where were you?" Lucille said. "I thought we'd lost you."

Three faces at the table grinned at me. A waitress stood at my elbow, a pad in one hand and a pencil in the other.

"Your order, sir?" she said.

I smiled and glanced at the menu. Dinner options at the roadhouse were limited. You could have anything you wanted as long as you wanted barbeque and beer. I ordered barbeque and beer. A transient combo played on a low platform across the floor. Various musicians came and went. A trombone departed, replaced by a trumpet. Later the trombone would return, and a clarinet would take a break. The music played on.

Couples danced on a small floor. The roadhouse wasn't the Shadowland Dance Club, and the Gage Brewer band wasn't in the house, but the intimate surroundings and the unrehearsed music suited me. The entire joint would fit in Richter's great room, but its setting offered more comfort than Richter's French provincial décor. I dubbed it early rustic.

"Mind if I dance with your gal, Pete?" Percival Gillman said and led Lucille from the table.

Agnes smiled at me, and I asked her to dance. We joined Percy and Lucille on the dance floor.

"I've never seen this side of Percy," Agnes said. "He's so relaxed, and he's having fun."

"He's away from the bank," I said. "He can be himself here. No one here knows he's a banker, and if they did, they wouldn't care. A guy can loosen the collar on his stuffed shirt in a place like this. Everyone is here to have a good time."

We danced to the voice of a long-legged beauty who crooned a haunting rendition of "Bye Bye Blackbird."

"Thank you, Pete."

I raised an eyebrow.

"For arranging this," she said.

"Arranging what?" I said. "Percy and I thought it would be fun to take our gals out on the town."

"You don't fool me," she said. "Percy didn't come up with this on his own, and you know it. You suggested this to him, and it was sweet of you. You knew I needed this. How did you put it? I have a lousy poker face."

I feigned surprise, but Agnes had me. I'd called Percy and put a bug in his ear. Like I told Agnes the day before, I had a lousy poker face, too. Our food arrived, and we returned to the table. We tucked into ribs, baked beans, and coleslaw. We sipped beer and listened to the music.

A number of musicians were present, and the informal makeup of the combo evolved throughout the evening. A brass or reed instrument appeared, then departed, and reappeared later. The improvised music, a mix of jazz and blues, entertained the lively crowd and never ceased.

We finished our dinner, and the waitress brought coffee. I slipped her a couple of bucks, and she returned with a pint of hooch wrapped in brown paper. We each added a dollop of brandy to our coffee. Onstage, a Louis Armstrong doppelganger blew a mean trumpet. A skinny kid who sported eyeglasses and a goatee played the drums. When the trumpet player exited the stage, another musician took his place and blew mellow notes on a saxophone. The kid wowed the crowd, a young man with talent beyond his years.

"That young man on the saxophone is terrific," I said. "I wonder if he's from around here."

Someone at the next table heard my comment.

"I heard that young man blow his horn in Kansas City," the man said. "His name is Charlie Parker. Folks call him Yardbird. He's just a teenager, but keep your eye on that cat. His music really stirs you, makes you want to boogie-woogie."

A wrinkled gal with graying hair and a cigarette scarred voice sang a passionate rendition of "Miss Brown to You." The audience rewarded her with polite applause, but no one mistook her voice for the pipes of Billie Holiday.

A gentleman at the microphone solicited the audience.

"Is there any talent in the crowd?" he said. "It's open microphone this evening. Here's your chance, ladies and gentlemen. Don't be shy. Come on up."

The crowd murmured, and I stood up.

"Right here," I said and pointed toward Agnes. "This lady has talent. She sings like a meadowlark."

Lucille giggled and applauded, and Percy patted Agnes on the shoulder. Agnes looked horrified, but Percy and I encouraged the applause, and others clapped and whooped. We urged Agnes to the microphone, and she relented. Onstage, she huddled with the musicians who nodded and began to play a lively tune. Agnes closed her eyes, waited for the downbeat, and eased into "My Melancholy Baby." Agnes wasn't Ella Fitzgerald, and she didn't pretend to be. She delivered the song in her voice, her style, and the crowd loved it. When the song ended, we clamored for more, and Agnes obliged. She sang three more tunes, then she bowed and blew a kiss to the audience, thanked the musicians, and floated back to our table.

"Pete, I wanted to strangle you," she said when she sat down. "I thought I would die of embarrassment. Then when I finished and everyone applauded, I thought I'd rather die than leave that stage."

She brushed away a tear with her napkin. We listened to music, polished off the brandy, and danced into the wee hours before we called it a night.

I woke up in Lucille's bed. I opened one eye, and Lucille smiled at me with both eyes opened and her hair brushed.

"How long have you been awake?" I said.

"Not long. Longer than you."

"Youth," I said.

"Pardon me?"

"You're younger by a decade. It's disheartening."

"Oh, pooh. I'll make coffee," she said. "That'll bring you out of your funk. After you open your other eye would you look at my lamp? It isn't working. It just needs a bulb change."

She got out of bed and went to the kitchen, and I padded down the hallway. After I visited the toilet, I found a light bulb in a closet. I also retrieved a basket I'd stashed away the night before and tucked it behind a pillow in the bedroom. The lamp was on her nightstand next to a radio. Before I removed the lampshade, I tuned in station KFH. Uncle Ben Hammond read the comic strips on Sunday mornings.

That morning, Uncle Ben's sidekick puppets, Hoots and Quacks, read the funnies with him. An over-the-fence neighbor teased Major Hoople about his expanding waistline in *Our Boarding House*. Mrs. Hoople loved to tease her husband and laughed when the Major got annoyed. In the next strip, Nancy and Sluggo tussled over an ice cream cone, and when it landed on the sidewalk, a puppy ate it. Hoots hooted, and Quacks quacked over that one. In *Blondie*, Dagwood was flummoxed when Elmo, the neighbor's kid, posed a question about the birds and the bees. Dagwood fumbled and stammered, and Elmo scratched his head. He didn't know what Dagwood was talking about. He just needed help on a science class project. They were studying birds and bees.

I changed the bulb and pulled the chain. No luck. The lamp didn't work. The tension on the chain didn't feel right. It didn't engage properly. I mumbled something to myself and returned to the closet for a screwdriver. Just change the bulb, a simple request. An uncle of mine once said that the most frustrating words in the world were, "All you gotta do is just . . ." I was disassembling the lamp when Lucille returned with coffee.

"Oh, I love Uncle Ben," she said and looked at the pieces of her lamp strewn across the cover of the bed. "I thought it just needed a bulb."

"No such luck," I said.

My screwdriver slipped and the blade gouged my thumb. My thumb trickled blood. Lucille wrapped the wound with a hankie. She shook her head and "tsked."

"I have a confession," I said.

"Is this where you tell me you don't really love me and you're only after my money?"

"You have money?"

That brought a tender jab from her elbow.

"No, it has nothing to do with money, and if you're after mine, you're in for a disappointment. This is worse. I'm not the man you think I am. I'm incompetent with tools. The smallest repairs stymie me. Give me a screwdriver, and I'm as hapless as an elk on ice skates. Give me a hammer, and I break things. Hand me a saw, and the board will be too short for the job. It's a curse."

She took the screwdriver out of my hand and put it on the nightstand. She gathered up the pieces of her lamp and placed them next to the screwdriver. She handed me a cup.

"Let's have coffee instead," she said.

I reached behind my pillow for the basket.

"What's this?" she said.

"Happy May Day," I said.

"Well, aren't you sweet? A May basket! I haven't had a May Day basket since I was a little girl."

She beamed at the pansies, the daisies, and the violets and the wrapped chocolates.

"Beautiful and delicious. Chocolate?"

I shook my head.

"My last May basket was in junior high school," she said. "You've brightened my day."

She kissed me on the cheek. Sunshine brightened the room. I usually left Lucille's place while it was still dark.

"You know, the sun is up," I said, "and my car is parked out front. Does that bother you?"

"You mean am I worried by what the neighbors will think?"

"Tongues wag," I said. "I don't want to cause a flap."

She grew thoughtful.

"There was a time, I suppose, when it would have bothered me. Not anymore."

She munched a chocolate, and I sipped coffee.

"Not since Sidney died," she said.

"Now you don't care?"

"No, that's not it. I care now more than ever, but only about what's important. It's different now. I lost my husband. I lost my friend Alice. That changed me."

Lucille's husband and her neighbor had each been murdered.

"After their deaths, I changed. In here."

She tapped herself on the chest.

"And in here."

She tapped her temple.

"Neighbors supported me through those awful days. They helped out, and I love them for it. I'm still grateful for their help. But neighbors gossiped, too. They wondered why Sidney was killed, why Alice died, too. They had questions. They put their heads together, talked to each other. They watched and whispered every time I left the house. It's only natural. The thing is, I quit worrying about what they said, and I don't worry about what they say today. I never will again. Now I concern myself with what's important. Behaving a certain way and trying to please others isn't important, at least not to me. I can't marry again, not yet. You understand that. That doesn't mean I don't want you to be in my life, Pete. I love you. If tongues wag, then let them wag. I have a life to live."

Lucille started to unwrap a chocolate, then dropped it back into the basket.

"Are you hungry?" she said.

"Starved," I said.

I reached across her to click off the radio.

"Let's start with dessert."

I kissed her on the neck, and she put her basket on the nightstand. I nibbled her ear. She smiled and came into my arms.

◆ ◆ ◆

17

A clock and a cloud.

Monday, May 2nd

The skies grew dark, and wind blowing out of the southwest kicked up dust and debris on the streets. Pedestrians scurried along the sidewalks in quick-step gaits, legs straight, knees locked. Men and women alike held onto hats with one hand and glanced at the sky toward the west. As my grandma used to say, it was coming up a cloud.

I sat behind the wheel of my roadster and dropped south on Waco to Douglas. I turned left and rolled east past my office in the Lawrence Block Building and pulled over to the curb in front of the Hotel Eaton near the intersection at St. Francis. I had raised the top to my roadster and snapped it into place earlier that day after visiting an old friend across town.

Before driving downtown from my place, I'd traveled to the northeast part of Wichita. Over the years, I'd done business with Doc's Clocks located at Twenty-First and Oliver. Many of the timepieces in my collection came from Doc's store, but on that day I picked up a clock Doc had repaired for me. He had found a new dome for my Austrian Zappler Animated clock to replace the one that had been cracked by the burglar in my home.

Doc was getting up in years, but his business kept him lively and spry, and I always enjoyed our visits. I found him that morning in his usual attire, white shirt and tie beneath a yellowing smock, pockets filled with small tools. His white hair hadn't been combed or brushed, but the eyes behind his spectacles were as bright as the smile beneath them.

"Come in, come in," he said when the bell tinkled above his door. "Your clock is in the back. Come with me."

I walked around the counter and followed him through the arched portal to the inner sanctum where he did his work. His workbench was covered with an array of small screwdrivers and wrenches. A clock lay open beneath a large magnifying glass mounted on a flexible arm. My Austrian Zappler Animated clock sat on the bench. Doc had not only replaced the dome, he had cleaned and polished the timepiece, too.

"It's a beautiful clock," he said. "Where did you get it?"

I told Doc about my visit to the curio shop in Hot Springs where I was entranced by the shop's owner, Carina, and where I fell in love with the clock I couldn't afford. Then, when I came into an unexpected windfall, I bought it.

"It's worth every penny," he said and began discussing interesting clocks he had owned or repaired. We talked, or rather he talked, and I listened for over an hour. He seemed grateful for the company, and I appreciated hearing his knowledge. As the morning dwindled, I paid him and thanked him. I drove to my place on Lewellen and returned the clock to its spot on the shelf before driving downtown.

The restaurant at the Hotel Eaton was packed with diners, every table occupied. I took a chair in the lobby and picked up a magazine. The hotel detective, a guy I recognized, walked by and caught my eye. He touched the brim of his hat, and I nodded. Patrons sat in wingback chairs or plush divans scattered between pillars and read newspapers or magazines. The pleasant aroma of pipe tobacco wafted through the lobby. I opened an issue of *The Atlantic Monthly* and scanned an article on William Butler Yeats, still writing poetry at the age of seventy-three according to the article. Good for him, I thought to myself.

I crossed my legs and noticed that my shoes could use a shine. The restaurant remained busy, so I rose from my chair and walked across the lobby. The clerk at the desk beamed as if I were the sole reason he came to work that day, but when I continued walking past the desk, he turned his attention toward another customer and offered an identical smile. My barber sat in the customer's chair reading the paper. I walked by, and he returned my nod through the window.

The shoeshine stand was situated in the hallway between the barbershop and the tobacco shop. The chair was empty. The shine man sat on a stool, elbows on his knees, and read from a book. He marked his place when I climbed up into the chair. I gazed down at his gray head and read the cover of the book he set aside, *Leaves of Grass,* by Walt Whitman. He looked up at me and grinned.

"Nice to see you, Mr. Stone," he said, "and from the looks of this leather, not a minute too soon. How're things in the detecting world? Tell me what you know."

"Well, Waldo, you'll be pleased to learn that your favorite Irish poet is alive and vital and still working at his craft into his seventies according to what I read."

"Yes, I read that article in *The Atlantic Monthly*," he said. "He's growing older, but aren't we all? Even youngsters like you and me."

Ellis Waldo laughed and daubed polish onto my shoes with his fingertips. He worked it deep into the creases of the leather, around the edges of the soles, not missing a spot. Waldo shined shoes like he did everything in his life, with gusto and skill, happy with his work and proud of it.

We'd known each other for years, and my admiration for him continued to grow. Early in life he'd learned that his dark skin led to closed doors, but he didn't succumb to bitterness. His short, formal education taught him how to read, and he developed a love for books as a child. That love never abated. Waldo discovered that books held the keys to doors that couldn't be slammed in his face. I wasn't surprised to learn that Waldo had read the article on Yeats. Waldo read everything he could find. He devoured the classics, poetry, history, science, philosophy, and the Bible. Waldo nurtured a keen mind that had matured through the decades into a fount of knowledge.

"Waldo, are you familiar with an organization called the German American Bund?"

When he heard the question, the shine rag that had blurred and popped paused over my shoes. Waldo looked up and shrugged.

"Why would you ask that?" he said. "Yes, I've read a piece or two about the German American Bund. I haven't read much about them, but then again I've read too much, if you know what I mean. You're curious about the Bund, but I know you're not planning to join them."

"You're right about that. I'm not looking for membership into their club."

"Well, I only know what I've read, and what I've read leaves me shaking my head in bafflement. I wonder what runs through some people's minds, if they bother to think at all. It's political in nature, the Bund is. They have their philosophy, I suppose, and some folks are attracted to it. We're all free to make our choices. Those who embrace the club's beliefs are welcomed into the fold, provided they are fair of skin and their religion agrees. As of yet, no one has extended an invitation to me."

He chuckled. A man strolled by the stand and spoke.

"Hello, Waldo," the man said.

The man's eyes met mine, and he saluted with two fingers to the brim of his hat.

"Good day, Mr. Bernstein," Waldo said. "Nice to see you."

Aaron Bernstein nodded and continued down the hallway toward the lobby.

"Now, there's a man who might answer your questions about the Bund," Waldo said.

"How do you know that man?" I said.

"Mr. Bernstein? He's a nice gentleman, staying in the hotel," Waldo said. "He stopped by my chair the other day. He visited the barber, too. Dapper gentleman, sharp dresser. He wears the finest shoes of imported leather."

I glanced at my shoes. They were made from the hides of homegrown cattle, and they were priced at less than four dollars a pair. Waldo caught himself and looked up. He seemed embarrassed by his comment about fine shoes and imported leather. I threw my head back and laughed. He shook his head and laughed, too.

"The gentleman read a copy of *The Kansas City Star* while I worked," he said, "but after a few minutes he tossed the paper aside and muttered, 'Disgusting.' That was the word he spoke. He'd read an article about that Bund group, he told me, and he also told me about plans for a national convention in New York City. He didn't say much more after that, but I could tell he was upset."

Waldo finished the shine and brought my battered four dollar shoes back to life. I thanked him for his usual fine job. We settled up and shook hands. I walked down the hall toward the front of the hotel and glanced at the patrons in the lobby. I thought I might spot Bernstein, but he wasn't there. The restaurant crowd had thinned, so I went inside to find a table. Thunder boomed outside. Through a window, I saw that the sky had darkened, and rain started to fall.

Bernstein sat at a table beside a window that looked out over the sidewalk along Douglas Street. He saw me enter and gestured at an empty chair across the table from his own. Thunder boomed again, the clouds opened, and rained poured. Pedestrians on the sidewalk darted for shelter. Raindrops splattered against the window. I sat down at the table, and the waitress arrived. Bernstein had already ordered. The waitress carried a tray that held a pot of coffee and two bowls of steaming chili.

"I hope you like chili. I like chili on a rainy day," Bernstein said, "something hot when it's dark and damp."

"One of my favorites," I said.

The waitress served the chili and poured coffee into cups. I sipped coffee and thanked the waitress. Bernstein crushed crackers into his bowl and wiped his hands on a napkin.

"You have a way of appearing and disappearing, in and out of the shadows," I said. "I see you, and then I don't. What should I make of that?"

"Beats me," he said, "What should you make of that?"

"The first time I spotted you was in this restaurant. You sat over there and read the sports page."

He glanced toward the table I indicated and nodded.

"We had this conversation at the Lassen," he said. "You were with a dame, and I read the sports page. Somebody alert the authorities. I eat here, and I sleep here. So what?"

"So, when I left that evening, you got up from your table and stepped into that telephone booth outside the door."

"I used the telephone," he said. "I do that from time to time. I call people. What I did not do was call a burglar at your home. You're acting paranoid, Stone. That's your problem, not mine, but if you want some advice, quit putting me under your magnifying glass. You're wasting your time. It could be we have similar interests."

Bernstein spooned his chili. My chili steamed, and so did I.

"Okay, we had this conversation at the Lassen," I said, "but the feds fed me a tale about you working with them. I don't buy it. I don't figure you, Bernstein. What similar interests do you and I have? What's your angle?"

"Eat your chili," he said.

The man was a puzzle. I ate my chili. Bernstein cleaned his bowl and lit a cigar.

"You have questions," he said, "and I have questions. We should talk, but now is not the time, and this is not the place. I have to be somewhere."

"Give me a time and a place," I said.

He looked out the window. The cloudburst had eased somewhat. The heavy rain turned into a steady drizzle.

"This storm will pass through. There's a ballgame tomorrow afternoon at the stadium down by the river. I'll get a box."

He stood up and reached for his wallet. I waved him off.

"The chili's on me," I said.

He nodded and put on his hat and left the table. I finished my chili and smoked a cigarette before I settled the bill. On the sidewalk, pedestrians hustled in the rain. The doorman recognized me and shrugged when I stepped outside under the awning. I gave him a "What are you going to do?" look and held the brim of my fedora with one hand. I stared at my shined shoes as I navigated the puddles on the sidewalk until I reached my building at the end of the block. A green bike leaned against a lamppost. Rusty delivered the afternoon edition of the newspaper, and he was chatting with Agnes when I entered the office.

"Atta boy, Rusty," I said. "Neither snow nor rain stays you from your appointed rounds."

"Huh?" Rusty said.

Agnes rolled her eyes.

"Mr. Stone is referring to the motto of our mail carriers," she said, "although, I think he butchered it a little. You're both soaking wet."

Agnes took a towel out of the closet and gave the lad's head a brisk rub.

"Rusty, dear, you'd better hurry along your appointed rounds and get home," she said. "You need to dry off before you catch a cold."

Rusty handed her a copy of the newspaper, and Agnes thanked him.

"You're welcome, Miss Agnes, and don't worry about me. I'm hunky-dory. It's just water. Maybe Mom will let me skip my bath tonight. See you, Mr. Stone!"

Out the door he went. I shook the water off my fedora, took off my coat, and hung them both up to dry.

"How about me, Agnes dear," I said. "Don't I get a towel and motherly advice?"

Agnes tossed the towel at me.

"I'm not your mother," she said, "and a man your age should know when to come in out of the rain."

18
Drowned frustrations.

Monday, May 2nd

"Sam Orsulak is lying. Martin Richter is hiding something. Darnell Pettigrew has gone missing, and I don't know what to think about Aaron Bernstein."

"Got it, Pete. I'm with you. Whatever you say is fine by me."

Tom placed a frothy glass of Storz beer on the bar in front of me.

"Understand, of course, that I have no idea what you're talking about," he said. "I don't know those men or what they did or didn't do, but as long as you are in my bar drinking my beer, what you say goes."

Tom moved away to serve another customer. The rain that had fallen all afternoon passed over the city and left a clear sky brimming with stars and a crescent moon in its wake. I sat on a barstool in Tom's Inn and nursed a beer and tried to drown my frustrations. It didn't work. It seldom did.

I used the foul weather that afternoon as an excuse to hole up in my office and make telephone calls. The excuse was legitimate, but the telephone calls proved to be fruitless. I was no closer to learning what information Cocky had obtained or why others were after that information than I was when the day began. I had a scorecard and a list of names, but so far, none of the players listed on the card had come out of the dugout.

Veatch told me over the telephone that he had talked to the FBI since my last visit, but he wasn't forthcoming on details of their conversation. He assured me that the feds did not update him on the status of their investigation, which made sense. The FBI wasn't known for discussing their work with civilians. Still, I sensed that Veatch didn't want to tip his hand to me, either. He wasn't sure if Cocky Wright figured into espionage, or even if espionage against Stearman existed, but what Veatch did know was my friendship and loyalty toward Cocky. Until I cleared my friend's name, Veatch wouldn't share everything he knew with me.

I questioned Veatch about Darnell Pettigrew's whereabouts. I hadn't heard from Pettigrew, and when I visited Stearman, he was not to be found. Veatch couldn't help me locate Pettigrew, but he connected me to the hangar, and I spoke to one of the mechanics who told me Pettigrew wasn't around.

"Come to think of it I haven't seen him since last week," he said. "He's probably down the road at Boeing. It's pretty quiet around here this afternoon. We were going to run flight tests, but they were called off because of the weather. Pilots can fly in the rain, but the guys on the ground wearing ties don't like to get wet."

That's the way the afternoon went. I telephoned Ethan Alexander at Wichita University and told him I'd attended the Forum luncheon he had recommended to me. I wondered if he knew anything about Martin Richter that might be helpful. He knew the name and was familiar with the man's politics, but other than disagreeing with those politics Alexander had little to add.

When the afternoon faded away, Agnes said goodnight, and soon after she left I locked the office door and drove over to Tom's Inn on Seneca where I sat atop a barstool. I glanced at my watch and calculated that I had been sitting on the stool for several hours. I noted the time, but I hadn't tracked the number of glasses of beer I drank. Tom finished with a customer and came my way.

"I don't know Pettigrew or Bernstein or those other fellows," he said, "so talk to me about something else. How about a bite to eat?"

I shook my head.

"Okay, let's talk baseball," he said. "Ask me what happened at Sportsman's Park today."

"What happened at Sportsman's Park today?"

"Funny you should ask," he said. "The Birds took the Cubbies six to three."

Tom grew up in the Missouri Ozarks, and he'd been a fan of the St. Louis Cardinals since he was a boy. A rivalry between the Cardinals and the Chicago Cubs had existed since the early days of baseball, and Tom relished the games when the Birds upended their rivals.

"Good for the Cardinals," I said. "Who pitched? Dizzy?"

I hoped he had some news on Dizzy Dean.

"The Cards went with Lon Warneke, and the Cubs went with Bill Lee," he said. "I'm glad the Cubs didn't use Dizzy Dean. I can't root for the Cubs, but I also can't root against Dizzy Dean."

Dizzy Dean had pitched for the Cardinals and been a longtime favorite of fans. That changed after the previous season came to a close, and he was traded to Chicago. Dean was dizzy, all right, an Arkansas hillbilly with a second grade education, blessed with a thunderbolt for an arm and a personality tempered with a sprinkling of yahoo craziness. He threw smoking hot seeds past the best batters in the game. On the field he was one of the greatest talents in the game. After the game when sportswriters crowded around for an interview, he enthralled them with his honest observations delivered in his unique, mangled mother tongue. Cardinal fans adored him.

It was not an injured arm that ended Dean's career. It was a broken toe. During the All Star game the summer before, a hard line drive came back to the mound and smacked Dizzy on his big toe. Trainers rushed to his side. When a medic informed Dizzy that his toe was fractured, Dizzy replied in typical fashion.

"Fractured, hell, the damn thing's broken!" he yelled.

His retort brought laughter, but the laughter died when Dizzy's fastball fizzled. He still threw hard, but the magic disappeared. He never regained his dominance after that. He struggled the rest of that year, and when team owners grew discouraged with his performance and the Chicago Cubs showed an interest, the Cardinals let him go. Fans in St. Louis were broken-hearted. They still loved the lummox, and they wanted to root for him, but no self-respecting fan of the Redbirds would root for the Cubs. He posed a dilemma.

"The game was close until the late innings," Tom said. "The Cubs took the lead in the eighth, but the Cardinals dropped a four-run bomb on them in the bottom of the inning. Medwick hit a two-run homer. Lon Warneke pitched the full nine for St. Louis. He even added a double himself. Not a bad day for the Arkansas Humming Bird. He made the Cubs pay for trading him to St. Louis."

I pointed at my empty glass, but Tom's wife, Mabel, appeared at my elbow and nixed the refill.

"No more beer, Tom. Pete's had enough," she said.

She took away the empty glass with one hand and placed a platter of food on the bar with the other. I protested.

"I'm not hungry," I said.

"Eat," she said.

Mabel had prepared a thick, juicy hamburger along with fried potatoes, coleslaw, and dill pickle spears. A dollop of spicy mustard rested atop the hamburger. The pleasant aroma of hot food wafted up from the plate. I spread the mustard with a knife and took a bite of hamburger. It was delicious, and I was ravenous. I said yum, and Mabel patted me on the arm. I wiped my mouth with a napkin and kissed the top of her gray head.

"Marry me, Mabel," I said. "Leave this bum, and run away with me."

"You've asked me to marry you before," she said

"I have?"

"Usually when I serve you food, and usually after you've been drinking. You don't remember because you've never asked me when you were sober."

Tom chuckled, and she rolled her eyes. We watched her toddle back to the kitchen. Tom poured a cup of coffee for me and another for himself. I ate my meal, and we drank coffee and smoked cigarettes. Tom and I talked baseball until he closed the tavern.

19

Baseball, bourbon, and the Bund.

Tuesday, May 3rd

At Market and Douglas, customers entered and exited the Fourth National Bank. Percival Gillman, bank cashier and Agnes's husband, came to mind. He'd let his hair down at the roadhouse Saturday night. He'd enjoyed the jazz and joy juice along with the rest of us, but as a bank officer he wore his collar starched and buttoned, ever diligent of his image in the community. Reputations of financial institutions had faltered in the wake of the '29 stock market crash and subsequent bank failures. Gillman strived to gain and maintain the trust and confidence of his customers, a mission he assumed with dedication. He placed a heavy load on his own shoulders. That quote from Jacob Marley's ghost popped into my head again. "I wear the chain I forged in life."

At Douglas and Main, two clerks in shirt sleeves and bow ties assembled a display of menswear in the window of Hinkels Dry Goods Company. An arrangement of dress shirts caught my eye. My own collar showed some wear. Maybe it was time to pay a visit to Hinkels.

I crossed the Arkansas River on Douglas, dropped south on McLean, and followed the winding drive along the riverbank to Lawrence Stadium at Maple Street. The white grandstands glistened in the sun. Red, white, and blue pennants fluttered in the breeze above the green rooftop. I drove into the lot and parked my roadster. A small crowd lined up at the ticket window, and I moved to the rear of the line. A young lad who'd been standing near the gate approached me.

"Are you with Mr. Bernstein, sir?" he said.

I nodded and said I was. The lady at the ticket window waved me in, and the boy ushered me through the gate. Lawrence Stadium was only four years old, but it had already developed its stately character. Instead of wood like most grandstands, this solid beauty was constructed with concrete. A project of the Civil Works Administration, it served as a site for baseball games and civic events. Franklin Roosevelt had delivered a campaign speech in the stadium a couple of years earlier. Local baseball teams such as the Wichita Watermen played in Lawrence Stadium, and semi-professional leagues used the site for a baseball tournament each year. That tournament included Negro teams, such as the Kansas City Colts, the Topeka Dodgers, and the Wichita Elks. Two of those teams were scheduled to play that afternoon. The Elks would host the Dodgers in a regular season game.

We reached the box seats, and the youngster waved off my tip.

"Mr. Bernstein took care of me," he said.

I thanked the lad and took a seat next to Aaron Bernstein. He nodded when I sat down, and we shared hellos. A mixed crowd of fans, light and dark faces, filed into the stands. It looked to be a sizable number of people for a midweek game. Bernstein buttonholed a peanut vendor who walked the aisle. The vendor leaned over, and Bernstein whispered instructions into his ear. The man bobbed his head, said, "Yes, sir!", and disappeared up the steps.

Bernstein pulled a humidor from his jacket pocket, held it toward me, and raised his eyebrows. I declined and lit a cigarette, and he removed a cigar from the humidor for himself. He produced a pearl-handled penknife from another pocket, snipped off the end of his cigar, and lit it with a gold lighter. He drew a satisfactory puff and blew a wisp of smoke into the cloudless sky.

"Great day for baseball," he said.

I agreed. The crowd was enthusiastic. Families and friends of players from Wichita and Topeka filled many of the seats. They raised their voices, taunted one another, and shared contagious laughter in a mood of celebration. Men and women sported finery, dressed to the nines. Men who wore dungarees to work every day had scrubbed away grease and dirt with calloused hands to don white shirts, bright ties, and creased trousers for the afternoon. Women wore their Sunday-go-to-meeting dresses along with hats adorned with feathers, ribbons, and bows. The game was baseball, but the atmosphere suggested a carnival. Animated fans hooted and hollered when their teams took the field, especially those with a son or a nephew playing in the game.

The peanut vendor returned to the box and handed a pair of drinking glasses to Bernstein. Bernstein passed a glass to me, amber liquid poured over ice. He tucked a folded bill into the vendor's shirt pocket and whispered again into the young man's ear. The vendor nodded and grinned and disappeared. Bernstein raised his glass in a toast.

"A great day for baseball," he said again.

The bourbon was smooth and warmed the body and soul. Bernstein had style, I had to give him that. He knew how to live. He wore a charcoal gray, pinstriped suit over a crisp, white shirt set off by a scarlet tie, matching silk pocket square, and a red carnation pinned to his lapel. Black and white two-toned shoes and a beaver fur fedora matched the suit and completed the ensemble.

"Bernstein, I'm a fan of the game," I said. "Ask anyone. There's nothing like baseball on a spring afternoon. Your seats are grand, your bourbon is delicious, and you're a gracious host. I'm not complaining, but tell me why we're here. I thought we were going to talk."

He crossed his legs and used the sole of his shoe to roll the ash of his cigar to a point.

"We are here to talk," he said. "I thought we should compare notes, take what you know and what I know, and see what it adds up to. Could be we could help each other. What better place than a ball game for a quiet chat? No prying eyes and ears, right out in the open. Look around. Most of the fans here are Negroes. There's no sign of the FBI, no sign of your Bund pals, either."

"My pals have nothing to do with the Bund."

"Noted. So, it's a good spot for a meet. Here we are sitting in the sun, just a couple of guys sipping bourbon and bumping gums."

"Okay," I said. "Let's divvy up the dope. Start with you. I don't swallow that malarkey about you being in league with the FBI. Baloney. You're connected, but not with the Italians. That name Bernstein doesn't have enough vowels in it to be Italian. You're with the Jewish mob. You're in Kansas City where you run numbers and gamble on sports."

"You've done your homework," he said and took a small ledger out of his pocket. "Yeah, I gamble. So, who do you like in today's game?"

"Forget it," I said.

He threw back his head and laughed and returned the ledger to his pocket.

"So, I did my homework," I said. "I'm a detective, and you're a mobster. Now what? Where does that leave us?"

He puffed on his cigar.

"You sound like you don't care much for me. Know a lot of men in my profession, do you?" he said. "What I do for a living is my business. I'm not here to talk about that. Why I'm in your town is my business, too, but that I'm willing to discuss."

"Fine. What draws a dashing blade like yourself to my town on the prairie? What's your angle with the FBI?"

"My people in Kansas City sent me here. My people talk, and I listen. As for the connection between the FBI and myself, at the moment we share common interests."

Common interests between the mob and the feds. That jibed with what Vinny had told me over the telephone. The FBI was working with the mob in the northeast to control smuggling operations.

"What are your common interests?"

"The feds are looking into the German American Bund. They don't like the Bund much, but their hands are tied, unless they discover that the Bund is up to something illegal. The feds think there's espionage in the aircraft industry, and they think the Bund is involved. They're suspected of funneling trade secrets back to Germany. As for my angle, as you put it, my people don't like the Bund much, either. Certain politicians in Germany and more than a few people in the Bund would like to do away with Jews. That doesn't sit well with us. We don't intend to sit back and let that happen, either. If it were up to me, I'd pop a few people behind the ear and go back home to Kansas City, but my orders are to work with the feds. That's what I'm doing."

"How does my dead friend play into this?" I said.

"The FBI suspects your pal sold secrets to the Bund."

"That's nonsense."

"I wouldn't know," he said. "I never met your pal. As far as I know, the feds don't have proof against your friend, but they know he attended meetings. His name is on a list of suspects. They think he had information that could incriminate some people in high places. Do you know anything about that?"

I considered the envelope and key Cocky left behind. Maybe that key unlocked secrets, but if it did, I didn't know what those secrets were. Bernstein looked toward the ball field. A batter had smacked a line drive that one-hopped off the fence. He raced around the bases and cruised into second with a standup double. Fans whooped, and a man a few rows back stood up and screamed, "That's my boy!" Other fans clapped and hollered. Even those rooting for the opposing team had to smile.

"Cocky Wright had nothing to do with the Bund, and I intend

to prove it," I said. "Even if he did attend their meetings, he never subscribed to their politics."

"How do you intend to prove that? What have you got?"

I studied Bernstein. He was a gangster, and I didn't condone his ethics, but he seemed to shoot straight with me. I pulled out my keychain and pointed to the key Sundown had found on her dresser.

"Keep this under your fedora," I said. "Cocky Wright left this on his dresser next to an empty envelope that had my name on it. I think he planned to tell me about the lock this key fits, but he died before that happened. All I have now is this key."

"That's not much of a key," Bernstein said. "It belongs to a small lock. What about the widow? What does she know?"

"She doesn't know a thing. Cocky wasn't the type to keep things under lock and key. She has no idea what it might open."

"A small key to a small lock. Not much of a clue."

"You're right," I said, "but whatever it leads to has important people feeling nervous, including one politician. That politician offered me a tidy sum of dough to cough up whatever I find, assuming I find anything at all. He thinks my pal had dope that must be important."

"You're speaking of Martin Richter," he said.

"Yeah, Richter. He tried to hire me, but I gave him the bum's rush. I don't care for him. I'm also trying to find my friend's boss, Darnell Pettigrew, but he's turned into a ghost. Everyone says he's around, but nobody's seen him."

A batter looped a single over first base, and the runner on second base flashed some speed. He rounded the corner at third and slid into home plate ahead of the right fielder's throw. A family to the right jumped to their feet and screamed. The batter's father laughed and yelled, "That's my boy! That's my boy!"

"What else have you got?" I said.

"Pettigrew is small potatoes," Bernstein said, "He's dirty, but he's small potatoes. He does what he's told. Still, the feds have him on their list, too."

The peanut vendor appeared with fresh drinks and handed them over. He left with a crisp bill in his pocket and a grin on his face.

"So, Pettigrew's dirty," I said. "I think he framed my friend. If he's a pawn, who's the king?"

"Don't get your hopes up, gumshoe. You won't be storming the castle in this backwater burg. If the Bund is involved, the king lives in a tower someplace far away."

I sipped my bourbon and considered Bernstein's words.

"That may be true," I said, "but if the plane crash that killed my friend wasn't an accident, then someone here in the Air Capital is responsible. Even backwater burgs harbor criminals. Everybody's got an angle. The feds are looking at espionage. You and your people are fighting discrimination against Jews. Yours truly just wants to clear his friend's name and deliver justice to those who sullied it."

Bernstein nodded.

"That sounds right. We have different interests, but our interests overlap. We can still help each other."

"Where does Martin Richter fit into the scheme of things?" I said.

"Martin Richter is a mouthpiece," Bernstein said, "maybe more. He's a politician, and he's effective. He'll sleep with anyone if it gets him what he wants."

"Funny you should mention sleeping with anyone. From what I saw in his home, it looks like he sleeps alone. The guy's wife is a beauty, but they sleep separately."

Bernstein grinned and sipped his bourbon. I lit a cigarette. We watched the game. The Wichita Elks won a nail biter, nine to eight. The Topeka Dodgers scored two runs in the final inning and had the tying runner on second base with only one out. The next batter hit a line drive up the middle, and the runner broke for third, but the second baseman dove to make a spectacular catch. He leapt for the ball and caught it inches off the ground. The base runner put on the brakes and spun back toward second base, but he was too late. Still on his knees, the second baseman lunged for the bag and tagged it ahead of the runner for the final out. The game ended on an unassisted double play. It reminded me of a play Cocky Wright had made when we played baseball together in our youth. I relished and relived the moment. The hairs on my neck stood on end. The family behind us screamed and jumped, and the father of the second baseman yelled over and over, "That's my boy! That's my boy!"

20

A smart guy.

Tuesday, May 3rd

A smart guy would have gone straight home. A smart guy would have gone home, heated up a bowl of soup, stretched back in his easy chair, and listened to the clocks tick while he mulled over what he'd learned from Aaron Bernstein. That's what a smart guy would have done, I thought to myself some time later. That was after I spent the evening on a barstool, chasing Bernstein's bourbon with several glasses of Tom's beer.

The inn had quieted down. A few fans had dropped in after the game for a beer and a bite to eat, but that crowd cleared out early. The next day was Wednesday, a workday and back to the grind. A family of six left the bar, and before the door swung shut behind them a few other people came in, men who had ended their shifts for the day and had an hour to kill. A pair of men sat in a booth along the wall and ordered from the kitchen. Another man took a stool at the end of the bar and stared into his beer.

I placed my keychain on the bar and laid the envelope that read 'STONE' alongside it. According to Bernstein, the feds had evidence that Cocky attended Bund meetings. That would explain those nights Sundown told me about when Cocky came home late and told her he'd been working extra hours. He hadn't been working late. He'd been meeting with the Bund. Why, I wondered? Tom refilled my glass.

"Where's your head tonight, Pete?" he said. "Talk to me. What's on your mind?"

I thanked Tom and sipped my beer.

"When I was a schoolboy I knew a kid, a smart kid," I said. "This guy always got the highest grade in the class, didn't matter what the subject was. He had brains, and he wanted to be a doctor. His dad was a doctor, and he wanted to be one, too. We all knew he'd become a doctor. After we finished school, he went back east to study medicine. That's what we thought, anyway. I figured he went to an Ivy League university. I didn't see him for several years.

"Our paths crossed again a few years ago, and by then he'd become a huge success. He lived in Kansas City, but we happened to meet here in town. He was staying at the Allis Hotel, and I spotted him in the lobby. We had lunch in the restaurant and caught up on what had happened since we were school chums. I could see by looking at him that he'd made it big. He drove a Cadillac and wore fine clothes. He showed me a picture of his wife and two kids, a beautiful gal and handsome youngsters. The man had the world by the tail on a downhill pull, and the man was miserable.

"Turns out he hadn't become a doctor after all. He wasn't smart enough, his words. He'd failed the entrance exams to medical school, and when he failed the exams he failed his father. His dad said he'd have to settle for something else, and when the word settle came out of his mouth, it was as if he'd tasted something foul. His father didn't berate him, not in so many words, but his tone said it all. Both of them, father and son alike, considered him a failure."

"So, your friend showed his old man, huh? What'd he do?" Tom said.

"He didn't come home with his tail between his legs. He stayed back east and studied engineering. Harvard refused him, so he went down the road to Boston Tech. He was always a whiz with numbers, and he fit right in with the slide rule crowd. Today he's a prominent engineer, recognized in his field. He designs bridges and buildings, big stuff. His dad never saw it, though. His dad died before he finished school, while he was still settling for something else. He never did show his old man. He's a brilliant engineer, but he washed out in medical school, and he still hears his father's ghost. He still thinks he isn't smart enough."

"What dredged up those thoughts?" Tom said.

"No one ever thinks he's smart enough, not even the smart guy. He knows that no matter how smart he is there's always someone smarter. Cocky was smart, but he doubted himself. He found something important, maybe evidence of espionage, so he took it to his superiors. Instead of congratulating him and slapping him on the back, his boss pointed the finger at him and accused him of crimes he didn't commit. Someone tried to frame him. Someone put incriminating photographs in his toolbox."

It had grown late, and the tavern was nearly empty. The pair of men seated along the wall settled their tab and left. The man at the end of the bar stepped into the telephone booth and placed a call, then he left, too. Tom and I were the only ones in the tavern. He washed glasses, and I stared at the keychain and the envelope on top of the bar.

"Cocky was smart," I said again. "Maybe he was too smart, too smart for me, anyway. The last time I saw him we sat right here on these stools and listened to the game on the radio. He was edgy and preoccupied that day. His mind wasn't here with us. He was thinking about something else. He'd already hidden whatever he had. He died the next morning before he could tell me what it was or where he hid it. That crash was no accident. Cocky died, but he left this key and this envelope. What do they mean?"

"Want my advice?" Tom said and didn't wait for a reply. "You're trying too hard. You've been staring at that key and that envelope all night. Back off. Relax. Quit studying and staring and let the answer come to you."

Tom was right. It was like trying to spot that star in the sky. If you stared right at it, it would fall into your blind spot, and you'd miss it. Cocky wouldn't hide anything near his family. Like a momma bird who leaves her nest and feigns an injury to draw a predator away from her fledglings, Cocky would draw his enemies away from the farm, away from his family. Nothing he hid was at the farm. He also wouldn't hide anything at Stearman. He didn't know who to trust at Stearman. Those thoughts haunted me. It wasn't on the farm, and it wasn't at Stearman.

Tom took away my empty glass and wiped off the bar.

"Let's call it a night, Pete," Tom said.

I nodded and looked again at the key and the envelope. A key and an envelope, an empty envelope with my name on it. I looked back and forth. A key. STONE. I thought about that final out in the game that afternoon at Lawrence Stadium. The batter hit a line drive up the middle. The runner at second base left the bag headed for third base. The infielder dove for the ball and caught it. Before the runner could return to second, the fielder slapped the base with his glove. An unassisted double play. Cocky Wright had made that same play when we were young. An unassisted double play. Key and STONE. Key. Stone. Key. Stone. Keystone. There it was. It hit me right on the chin. Keystone. From beyond the grave, Cocky spoke to me. I heard his words almost as if he sat on the stool next to me. Keystone.

"I've got it, Tom," I said. "I know where Cocky hid it."

Tom placed his forearms on the bar and leaned forward.

"That's great," he said. "I knew you'd figure it out. I'm sure there's a terrific story to go with it, and I want to hear every word of it, but not tonight. Tonight I'm bushed. Let's go home, and tomorrow night you can tell me all about it."

I nodded. That sounded like a good idea. I'd had enough to drink, and I needed some shuteye. Tom would hear the story soon enough. That was the plan, to go home, but did I mention that a smart guy would already have been at home? A smart guy wouldn't have gone to the tavern at all that night. A smart guy would have gone home from the stadium after the final out and had a nice, warm bowl of soup. That's what a smart guy would have done.

21
The last chip.

Tuesday, May 3rd

The sky was overcast, and the streetlights were dim. Tom and I said our goodnights on the sidewalk. He locked the door to the tavern, and I strolled toward my roadster parked down the block. Shadows covered the walk. I took my keychain out of my pocket and sensed movement in the shadows. Something solid jabbed me in the back.

"Do you know what this is?" a voice said.

The owner of the voice poked me again. Even a brain soaked in bourbon and beer recognized the barrel of a gun.

"I have an idea," I said.

"Good. I heard you were a smart guy. Listen carefully, smart guy. Don't do anything sudden like. Just keep walking. Go straight ahead up the sidewalk. While you're at it hand over those keys, and don't turn around when you do it."

I held up the keys, and a hand snatched them from behind. The barrel nudged me, and the three of us walked single file, me, the gun in my back, and the voice in the shadows in that order. At the end of the block we reached a Chevrolet coupe parked at the curb. The voice ordered me to open the passenger door, so I did.

"Get in," the voice said.

"Is this the part where you blindfold me and drive me to your secret hideaway?"

"Don't get wise. Get in the car and slide over behind the wheel. You drive."

He ordered me to drive, no blindfold and no secret destination. That meant a one way trip for the smart guy. We'd drive there together, but he'd drive away alone. I got in and slid over behind the wheel, and he sat in the passenger seat.

"Drive," he said.

We rolled north on Seneca. The late night traffic was light. Most homes we passed had gone dark for the night. We reached the intersection with McLean, a boulevard that ran along the bank of the Arkansas River. The voice instructed me to turn left. I looked both ways for traffic and glanced at the face in the shadows. I couldn't make out his features. It didn't matter. I knew who it was.

"Keep your eyes on the road," he said.

"We haven't introduced ourselves," I said. "We should introduce ourselves, don't you think? We were together all evening, and you never said a word to me. That was you, wasn't it Pettigrew, sitting there at the end of the bar? You should've spoken up. I'd have bought you a beer. We could have chatted. Now, without even a by your leave, you point the business end of that heater at me and give me orders. Is that any way to act? Why the mystery, Pettigrew? What are you hiding?"

"Zip your lip and drive, smart guy."

"We could stop for a nightcap. Hash it out over a drink."

"I said drive."

I drove along the river. At Central he waved the tip of his gun, and I turned left. A couple of cars passed by going the other way, but there were no pedestrians and few lights burning at that hour. Businesses and homes were dark. A siren sounded behind us. Pettigrew tensed and looked over his shoulder. I pulled to the right and slowed, and an ambulance sped by us and disappeared into the night.

"You seem edgy, Pettigrew. Why's that? This isn't your first murder, is it? You're an old hand at this. You killed Cocky Wright, didn't you?"

"Cocky Wright died in an airplane crash, an accident."

"We both know that's not the full story. Someone made that crash happen. Was it you?"

"Shut up. Turn right here."

I turned north on Sheridan and we rumbled over the railroad tracks. Dim lights glowed in a few homes. Most were dark. The sparsely populated neighborhood near the edge of town was not fully developed, and empty lots separated homes.

"Right here," Pettigrew said. "Pull in the drive."

I turned onto a gravel and dirt driveway and rolled to a stop near the closed door of a garage. An unlit house stood to the right of the driveway. Pettigrew opened his door.

"This way, real slow," he said.

He kept his gun on me while I slid across the seat and exited through the passenger door. We stood face-to-face in the shadows near the house. Clouds in the overcast sky had parted and revealed a partial moon.

"Waxing crescent," I said.

"What're you mumbling about?"

"Waxing crescent, the phase of the moon. Not more than a fingernail now, but it's growing."

I couldn't see his eyes, but I imagined he rolled them. I sounded breezy, but it was an act. The man had a gun, and the gun was pointed at me. He intended to use it, but he wanted to talk first. Pettigrew wanted information, and until he got that information, I stood a chance of seeing the sun rise on another day.

"Inside," he said. "The door's unlocked. Go slow. There's a light switch inside the door. Use it."

I climbed two steps onto a small landing and opened the door, a side entrance into the house. I flipped the switch and stepped into a kitchen with Pettigrew and his gun right behind me. The kitchen was bare except for a coffeepot on the stove and fixings on the countertop. The sink held empty cups. A bare wooden table with straight-backed chairs had a dirty ashtray filled with dead cigarette butts sitting on it. The walls were undecorated, and smart money would bet the cupboards were bare, too. A shoddy curtain covered a lone window in a corner of the room. An icebox stood in another corner, but there was no sign of food anywhere. No dishes, cutlery, or towels, not even a breadcrumb could be seen. Someone used the house, but no one lived in it. A mouse in the house would have relocated.

"This is real nice, Pettigrew. I love what you've done with the place."

"Shut up," he said.

It was getting to be his pet phrase. He pulled a chair out from the table.

"Sit," he said.

He didn't drag me to that house and that kitchen just so he could plug me, not yet anyway. All he'd have for his trouble would be a bloody mess. That made no sense.

"I've had a few beers," I said. "Give a guy a break. Let me use the gent's first."

"Open your coat," he said.

I opened my coat, and he eyeballed me right and left to make sure I wasn't carrying a gun. I wasn't. He waved his pistol toward the hallway and instructed me to flip a light switch. We walked past a living room whose Spartan décor matched that of the kitchen. Straight-backed chairs made up its only furnishings. A pair of doors in the hallway were pulled shut, but the door to the bathroom at the end of the hall stood open. I pulled a chain that lit a bare bulb and started to close the door.

"Eh, eh, eh," he said.

I left the door open, and he stood behind me in the hallway while I did my business. I flushed the toilet and rinsed my hands at the sink, but of course there was no towel, so I shook my hands and wiped them on the front of my shirt. We went back to the kitchen, and he kept his gun on me while he dragged the chair next to a radiator on the wall.

"Sit down," he said.

I sat, and he produced a set of handcuffs from his coat pocket. He tossed the bracelets at me.

"One on the radiator, one on your wrist."

I did what he said. I was chained to the radiator with one hand free, but there wasn't a thing within reach worth grabbing. He sat down at the table, close but not too close, and took my keychain out of his pocket. He slapped it on the table.

"Talk," he said.

"Those are my keys," I said. "What else do you want me to say?"

"Don't be a wise guy. You been staring at those keys all night long. They mean something. You had an envelope, too. Toss it on the table."

I fished the envelope out of my coat pocket and flipped it onto the table. He set it next to the keys.

"Stone," he said, "all in capitals. What does that mean?"

"Well, it could be that that's my name and the envelope was meant for me, but that's just a stab in the dark. What do I know? I could be wrong."

The hand came quickly and with force. Pettigrew's open palm slapped me against the head and rang a bell. Just as quickly the hand was gone and he was back in his chair.

"That's a taste," he said. "Every time you crack wise or give me an answer I don't like, you get one of those. Now, wise guy, what about the keys and the envelope?"

I shook my head and rubbed my jaw with my free hand.

"Mind if I have a cigarette?"

He made a motion with his gun, and my free hand fumbled in my pocket for cigarettes and matches. I took a drag and flicked an ash onto the floor. I didn't think Pettigrew would mind, and I was right. He didn't.

"The envelope is an envelope, nothing more. It's just the way I received it, my name printed on the front and nothing but empty air inside. Cocky Wright left it on the bureau in his bedroom. His widow found it and gave it to me after he died. I don't know what he intended to put in the envelope and neither does his widow. Maybe he never intended to use it at all. Maybe he meant to tell me something instead, but he never got the chance. We planned on having dinner together later that week, but those plans died when he did."

He mulled that over, but not for long. His brain pan wasn't overly developed.

"What about the keys?"

"What about the keys? They're my keys. What else can I say?"

That brought another slap. He used his palm again, and the bell rang again, but he didn't use his fist. He didn't want to knock me out. He just wanted my attention. He meant to keep me conscious.

"You stared at these keys all night," he said. "They mean something."

He held them up one at a time so I could identify them one at a time.

"My office door. My house. My car."

He held up the small key. Pettigrew had left the bar before I had my Eureka moment. He didn't realize the significance of the key. Tom was the only person in the room when I yelled I've got it.

"That goes to a jewelry box."

"What's in the jewelry box?" he said.

"Not much. Cufflinks, tie bars, a pocket watch, maybe a few coins."

"This isn't much of a key," he said.

"It isn't much of a jewelry box."

He slapped me again.

"What was that for?" I said.

"That's because I don't like your answers."

He stood up and moved to the stove. Neither of us spoke while he brewed a pot of coffee. He glanced at me, then went down the hall to use the toilet. He didn't bother closing the door. When he returned and the coffee was ready, he rinsed a dirty cup under the tap, filled it with coffee, and sat back down at the table. The coffee smelled delicious, and he seemed to enjoy it. I wasn't invited to have a cup.

"You're lying," he said. "I want to know what you've got."

"I've got nothing, Pettigrew."

He slapped me again.

"I'm getting tired of that, Pettigrew. Quit using your hand and use your head. You think Cocky Wright had something important, something that could make things go bad for you if the cops got ahold of it. You think I know what that is. You think I have something. Well, if I had anything, you and I wouldn't be having this conversation. If I had anything, I'd have coughed up the goods to the cops. I'd be at home right now, nestled in my nest, and you'd be behind bars."

His eyes never left mine when he sipped his coffee and lowered his cup.

"Maybe you're telling the truth. Maybe not."

That covered the options. The guy was a genius all right.

"What are you involved in?" I said. "What was my pal up to that has you so nervous? Who do you work for? The Bund?"

His jaw tightened.

"What do you know about the Bund?" he said. "I thought you said Wright died without talking."

"He wasn't the only one interested in the Bund," I said. "That band of cutups has caught the attention of the feds, too, not to mention the executives who sign your paycheck. You must know that. I figure this charming hideaway we're sitting in is your little clubhouse, isn't it? Am I right? Is this where you and the boys in the Bund play your little games? Is this where you do your deals, where you sell photographs and trade secrets? How about it, Pettigrew? What are you up to and who do you work for?"

He got red in the face. He swiveled in his chair and threw his coffee cup against the wall. A few shards landed in the sink. He stood up and stuffed the envelope and my keys into his pocket. He tossed the key to the handcuffs at me.

"Let's go," he said.

I unlocked the bracelets and stood up.

"Get in the car."

I led the way with the gun poking me in the spine. He flipped the light switch and closed the door. We stepped off the landing and repeated our routine, me behind the wheel while he took the passenger seat. I backed out of the driveway.

"Where to?" I said.

"South. Take McLean to Douglas then over to Broadway."

We drove in silence. Pettigrew was through talking. He'd let his heater talk for him. I considered my options. They were few and lousy. We rolled east on Douglas across the river, and after a half dozen blocks we reached Broadway. Downtown was dark. I hoped to spot a patrol car, but my luck held. It stayed rotten. The streets were dead. We went south on Broadway. Maybe Pettigrew would direct me to Stearman on Oliver. Maybe he planned to leave my body at the edge of town, or maybe he'd toss it off the John Mack Bridge into the Arkansas River. The river cut through Wichita along the west side of downtown then wound around the south side of the city. Broadway would cross the river south of Pawnee near the city limits. I decided to act before then. We reached Waterman, and I asked a question.

"Do you play poker?" I said.

We went through the intersection, and I eased my foot down on the gas pedal.

"Slow down," Pettigrew said.

I ignored him.

"Poker. Ever play poker?" I said.

"Poker? What're you talking about? Slow down, I said!"

I sped up. We approached the intersection at Kellogg. A driver in a westbound car tooted his horn and slammed on the brakes.

"Yeah, poker. In a poker game, who's the guy you've got to worry about, Pettigrew, the guy to look out for if you want to stay in the game? You want to keep playing, don't you? So, who do you have to keep an eye on?"

"I don't know. Slow down, I said. Do it now."

His eyes flicked toward me, then out the window, then back at me. He kept the gun pointed at me, but his back was scrunched tight against his door. The streets were empty. I ignored the signals and blew by the intersections.

"Play along, Pettigrew. Who's the guy at the table you should watch out for?"

"I don't know!" he said.

He wasn't looking at me now. He watched the store fronts and telephone poles whizz by.

"Slow down!" he yelled.

The blocks went by in a blur. Lincoln and Harry were the major intersections, and we breezed through those without slowing down. I watched the road, and I watched Pettigrew. I ignored the speedometer. The intersection at Levy lay ahead. Pettigrew wanted to plug me, but it was too late. We were traveling too fast for that. If he shot me, the car would crash. It would be suicide for him. We'd both end up dead.

"Who is it, Pettigrew? Who's the scariest player at the table?"

He screamed his answer.

"The guy with the chips! He's the guy to watch. The big winner! Watch out for the big winner! The guy with all the chips!"

"Wrong, moron. The guy to be afraid of is the guy with nothing to lose, the guy who's down to his last chip. That guy is scary. That guy will do something crazy. He'll do anything to stay in the game, and he's got nothing left to lose."

The John Mack Bridge loomed ahead. I edged the right wheels off the road. The car rumbled over the uneven surface. Pettigrew's eyes grew wide. He pulled his feet beneath him and squatted on the seat. He held the gun in his right hand with his left arm wrapped around his knees. He spoke, and his voice cracked.

"What are you doing? Are you crazy?"

"I'm not crazy, Pettigrew. I'm just down to my last chip."

I braked hard, and the car skidded. I cut the wheel to the left. The Chevy would have rolled if hadn't been for the bridge. The car slid sideways and slammed into the structure, crashing at the juncture of the first arch and the abutment. Metal, rubber, and glass met solid concrete, and bits of debris flew in all directions. The crash was loud, but it didn't mute the blast from the gun. The passenger door folded inward, and a heavy weight hurtled toward me and threw me against the other door. Shards of broken glass slashed my scalp. Twisted metal shuddered and hissed and rocked to a stop. Debris settled. The crumpled heap of flesh that had once been Pettigrew lay on top of me, half on, half off the seat. I pushed against the heap, and got nothing but sharp pains for my efforts. My keys fell out of his pocket and landed on my chest. I wrapped my fingers around the keys. My voice came as a hoarse whisper.

"Keystone," I said and faded into black.

22

Tell her to marry a banker.

Thursday, May 5th

Well, you're back."

The voice was feminine and unfamiliar. I turned my head and groaned.

"Lie still," the voice said, and the head of the bed rose several inches.

"Here," she said and placed a straw in my mouth. I drew a swallow of water and fell back on the pillow. She wore a white dress. A hat with a dark horizontal stripe was perched atop her gray head. She leaned closer when I spoke.

"Where am I?"

"Wichita Hospital," she said. "You were in an auto accident, according to the ambulance driver, and you looked it. Your head was a bloody mess, but your cuts were only scalp deep, lucky for you. The doc stitched you up. Your head is bandaged. It'll be some time before you cut a dashing figure, but you didn't suffer brain damage. I wonder if you have a brain anyway. How fast were you driving?"

The nurse was direct, all business. I liked her. I nodded toward the water glass, and she held the straw for me again.

"How about a cigarette?" I said.

"I don't smoke, and if you had cigarettes in your pocket, they didn't survive the crash. Your personal effects are in the drawer there."

She indicated a nightstand next to the bed.

"Why don't you settle for breakfast instead?" she said. "I can rustle up some eggs and coffee."

"Coffee sounds good," I said. "Is it morning yet?"

"Yes, it is morning, but not the morning you think it is. Today is Thursday. You missed Wednesday, slept right through it. Don't worry. You weren't in a coma. The doctor put you under so he could stitch your scalp and ordered medication to help you sleep. He figured rest was the best medicine. He was right."

I tried to sit up and groaned again. The nurse told me to lie still, and she raised the bed to a sitting position. I looked around the ward. My bed was next to a window, and on the other side was another bed, empty. The next bed held a patient who seemed to be sleeping.

"You've got plenty of bruises, but no broken bones," she said. "The bruises will heal with time and rest. Your passenger wasn't so lucky, I'm afraid. He didn't make it. I'm sorry."

"Don't be," I said.

She nodded and waited several seconds before she spoke.

"They said they recovered a gun at the scene, and the doctor said you had an unusual wound on your right thigh."

My hand moved to the bandage on my leg.

"The wound looked like a burn or a scrape, and there was that gun. Maybe a bullet grazed your thigh. If that's the case, you are one lucky man. If you survived a crash that horrific and a bullet wound to boot, you must be blessed."

She waited for a response, and when she didn't get one she promised to return with nourishment.

"Hurry back," I said. "After breakfast I intend to ask you to marry me."

"Not me, sailor," she said. "You're too ugly and stupid for this old gal."

She squeezed my hand and smiled when she said it. She left, and I lay back on my pillow and closed my eyes. Soon after, I heard another feminine voice, one that was familiar.

"Oh, Pete," she said.

Lucille's eyes were moist. She bent over and kissed my forehead.

"Please tell me you feel better than you look," she said.

"Sorry, doll. If I look anything like I feel, you might as well get the shovel."

She tried not to cry. She failed.

"You shouldn't joke," she said.

"I'll be fine, Lucille. Don't cry. A bad man wanted to kill me. I didn't let him. I'm still here, and he's not. End of story."

"Yes, end of story. That's what you always say, isn't it? Except it never is the end of the story, Pete. There's always another bad man, another bullet, another accident, and then what?"

The nurse returned with a tray in her hand and placed it atop a rolling table on an arm that extended over the bed. Lucille turned to leave, but the nurse shook her head.

"Stay, sweetie," she said and pulled a chair from the foot of the bed to the side. "He could use your company."

The nurse left. Lucille spoon fed me scrambled eggs and held my cup while I sipped coffee. After a few bites and several sips, I lay back. I didn't remember closing my eyes, but I must have napped. When I opened my eyes, Lucille was gone and so was the nurse. I needed a toilet. There was a bedpan on a stand next to the bed, but I ignored it. I managed to sit up and drop my legs over the side of the bed. A shuffle across the floor led me to a door that opened into a bathroom. I shouldn't have glanced in the mirror. I looked better than Boris Karloff's mummy, but the nurse was right. I was ugly. I finished my business and shuffled back to the bed. I opened the drawer in the nightstand and removed my wallet, my notebook, and my keychain.

I stared at the keychain for a moment and looked around for my clothes. I had to leave. I didn't see my clothes and figured they hadn't survived the crash. The medics probably removed them with scissors. My shoes were under the bed, and I slipped them on. I opened the door and stepped into the hallway. A uniformed cop sat in a wooden chair that was tipped back on two legs leaning against the wall. He looked at me and at my bandaged head. I wore a hospital gown and unlaced oxfords, and I held my personal effects in one hand. He shook his head.

"Well, damn," he said. "You just cost me five bucks."

I raised my eyebrows.

"McCormick said you'd do something stupid. He said you'd try to bust out of here without the doc's say so, but I said no way, the guy's too beat up to leave under his own steam. I told him it was a waste of time, ordering me sit here and watch that door. Mac just shook his head and said five bucks. Dummy that I am, I took the bet. Stupid me. Okay, Stone, let's go. McCormick wants to talk to you."

The cop was good-natured about losing the bet. He agreed to drive me home so I could put on some clothes before delivering me to Lieutenant Thaddeus McCormick, homicide detective. We drove north from the hospital located at Seneca and Douglas. In a few blocks we rolled past my roadster parked at the curb near Tom's Inn. The cop promised he'd deliver the car to me at the station, a decent gesture. At my place on Lewellen, he didn't complain when it took me several minutes to button my shirt and tie my tie, and he got a kick out of my clocks chiming the noon hour, twelve times in unison. We drove to police headquarters and chatted about baseball. All in all, the cop took everything a lot better than McCormick did.

"So, I come into the station Wednesday morning, I pour myself a cup of coffee, and before I take my first sip the desk sergeant buttonholes me. He tells me we've got a body lying in the morgue, and he tells me you're in the hospital. He tells me a pile of wreckage that was once a car is wrapped around the John Mack Bridge. I listen and say fine, it's an auto accident, no business for a homicide detective. Then he says the medics found a gun at the scene, and our guys found a bullet buried into the floorboard of the wreckage. Now, we don't know what we've got. We've got one dead and one injured. Is it an accident or a homicide? We're left with questions. The guy in the morgue isn't talking. That leaves us with you, a two-bit detective who looks like he's banging on the door of the morgue his own self, dying to get in. What's going on, Stone? Talk to me."

"I resent your two-bit detective reference, Mac. I'm cheap, but I'm not that cheap."

"You look like hell," he said. "Who's the stiff?"

"The stiff's name is Darnell Pettigrew."

"We got that from his wallet."

"Pettigrew was employed at Stearman Aircraft."

"Stearman, huh? Isn't that where the plane crash occurred, the plane that went down with your pal?"

I nodded.

"I'm sorry about your pal," he said. "Any connection between that plane crash and the crash at John Mack Bridge?"

Mac and I talked. Rather I talked, and he listened. I sat in a straight-backed chair in the office of Detective Lieutenant Thaddeus McCormick at the city's Central Police Station, a spiffy structure abutted to City Hall at the corner of William and Main. The building had once housed the fire department, but it became police headquarters when New Deal dough allowed the city to redo it in the latest Art Deco style. I sat across the desk from Mac. He puffed on a cheap cigar, and I opened a fresh pack of cigarettes bought on the drive from my place with my cop chauffeur. We blew smoke and shared stale air.

The building had a facelift, but Mac looked the same, a little pinker on top and heavier in the jowls since I'd last seen him. His gangly frame, a loose assemblage of lengthy limbs, knobby knees, and elbows akimbo lent an ungainly appearance. The guy would lose a beauty contest to a walnut tree, but he was a good cop, tough but measured. We formed a mutual respect over the years, but he came down hard when I gave him a headache. I often gave him a headache. He poured the sludge that passed for coffee at that place and handed me a cup. It tasted like Arkansas River mud. I drank every drop.

I told the story, what I knew. I also shared my suspicions about Cocky's death not being accidental. Mac listened with his arms atop his desk. He leaned forward and heard every word. He studied me like a grandmaster studied a chessboard. I mentioned meeting the FBI at Stearman, and he raised his eyebrows.

"The FBI stopped by the station to see the chief. Courtesy call. They offered no details about what they're doing in town, but they wanted him to know they were here."

I told him about my encounter with Pettigrew outside of Tom's Inn, how I'd been kidnapped at gunpoint and forced to drive the car, presumably to my execution. That resulted in the crash. I finished, and he shook his head.

"I don't know what you're mixed up in, Stone, but watch your back."

"Thanks, Mac. Nice to know you care."

He swept the air with the back of his hand, and I left. Outside his office, the cop who had driven me from the hospital handed me my keys.

"It's parked out front," he said.

I took my keys from him and fished a five dollar bill out of my wallet. I handed the bill to the cop.

"What's this for?" he said.

"I lost a bet," I said. "I told Mac there were no decent cops left in the city."

My roadster was parked out front, just as he'd said. I glanced at my watch. Cocky stashed the goods, and I intended to retrieve them, but I'd have to drive out of town to do it. The afternoon was dwindling, and my body ached, and my head throbbed. I drove a block north to Douglas and four blocks east to Emporia. I parked at the curb near the Lawrence Block building.

Agnes sat at the typewriter. The keys stopped clacking, and she stared when I walked through the door. I put my hat on the rack and shuffled to my office. A moment later she came in with two cups of coffee. She put a cup on the desk and pecked me on the forehead. Her eyes were misty.

"I guess this is my day to get kissed on the head by teary-eyed women," I said.

"Pete, Pete. I won't lie to you. You look awful. Why are you here? Go home and get some rest."

"I will. I wanted to check in first."

"Lucille called. She said you walked out of the hospital. Not released. Walked out."

"I planned on going for a drive, but I was waylaid by the police."

Agnes fingered a cameo locket she wore on a chain around her neck. I used it to change the subject.

"Is that new?" I said.

"Isn't it beautiful? It belonged to Percy's mother. He forget he even had it. He found it in a jewelry box and gave it to me. I just love it."

"You look lovely," I said.

"I wish I could say the same about you," she said and sat down across the desk from me. "Lucille is worried to death about you. She sat at your bedside most of the day yesterday. I worry about you, too. You almost died, Pete."

"The doc says get some rest, and I'll be good as new."

"And look at how you listen to the doc. Go home."

"What is it with women?" I said.

She set her coffee cup on my desk and fingered her locket.

"Women pay attention," she said. "We watch out for the men in our lives, especially those men who don't take care of themselves, which is all of you. It's the way we are. Women learn to look after their men, usually by example. Somebody has to look after you. Men never grow up. You keep that little boy inside of you. You wear masks and capes, swing swords and kick in doors, all-powerful and invincible. Well here's a bulletin. You're not invincible."

She stopped speaking and dabbed her eyes with a handkerchief.

"I'm fine, Agnes," I said. "I had a close call, but I'm fine. Don't worry."

"Yes, you're fine," she said, "this time. Maybe you'll be fine the next time, too, but what happens when things go sour and you don't come back? Then what?"

I let that question hang in the air.

"Go easy with Lucille, Pete. Be gentle. She lost a husband. She might not survive if anything happens to you."

"I plan on being around for some time."

"Of course you do," she said. "You all do. Lucille knows what you do for a living. There's an excitement, even a thrill, knowing that her man slays dragons for a living, but that thrill dies quickly when her man faces real danger. Lucille doesn't want anything to happen to you. She doesn't want to be alone. Sometimes a woman craves the humdrum, the routine. She's willing to give up a certain amount of excitement. She likes a husband who comes home every day."

"I'll go easy and be gentle," I said. "Thanks for the advice. What should I say to Lucille?"

Agnes picked up her coffee cup and rose from her chair.

"If Lucille wants a quiet life with humdrum and routine, tell her to marry a banker."

She winked at me and left the office.

23
Keystone.

Friday, May 6th

Gray dawn crept in before exhaustion departed. I lay in a vapor, drunk with sleep. Dreams edged into consciousness, and consciousness ebbed into dreams. I drifted and bobbed atop drowsy waves, not yet awake, no longer asleep. An apparition glowed and formed a shape, an archway. A woman took my arm, and together we passed beneath the arch. A crack of a bat and the blur of a baseball. A diving catch. A fan yelled, "That's my boy!" A dog barked. A prairie sky on a moonless night. A star not visible, lost in my blind spot. Look to the side. An unassisted double play. That's my boy. A key. An envelope. STONE. STONE and a key. Let the star come to you. STONE. Key. STONE. Keystone. There it was. The star shone and blinked, right where it had been all along.

My eyes opened and adjusted to the dim light. A screen door slammed. A car's engine turned over. I moved and ached when I did, but I moved easier that morning than I had the night before, and I ached less, too. I swung my legs over the side of the bed and sat in the quiet gray for several moments. The clocks chimed and bonged seven times in unison.

I padded to the bathroom and gazed at the ogre in the mirror. The ogre gazed back. Neither of us smiled. Some of the bandages on my head had loosened in the night. I secured them as best I could. Following a shave and a bath, the ogre was no Prince Charming, but he'd have to do. I dressed in khaki slacks and a chambray shirt and moved to the kitchen. I drank coffee and smoked a cigarette. Then I went down the stairs, rummaged in the shed for a shovel, and tossed it into the back of the roadster. I drove west out of the city onto the dusty country roads.

Cocky left me a signal. I caught his signal in Tom's Inn just before Pettigrew kidnapped me and we had our encounter with the bridge. The key and stone. Keystone. I knew Cocky wouldn't hide anything on the farm close to his family, and I knew he wouldn't hide anything at Stearman. He'd hide it in a place where only I would find it. Keystone was the clue. An archway had a stone at the top that held it together. Architects and builders called it the keystone. That's also the position second base held on a baseball diamond, the base at the top of the arch. Ballplayers referred to second base as the keystone sack, Cocky's position on the field. That was the signal Cocky left, a key and my name on an envelope, Stone. Whatever Cocky hid was near second base.

I slowed the roadster and rolled to a stop. The road was blocked by a herd of sheep. A farmer and his shaggy dog drove the sheep from a wheat field toward a pear orchard across the road. The farmer waved when he strolled in front of the roadster, and I returned the wave. Down the road a meadowlark warbled on a fence post, and another meadowlark on the next post returned the call.

Cocky and I played on dozens of baseball fields over the years, but there was only one that mattered that day, the one where it all began. A car passed going the other direction. The driver waved like folks did in the country, and I waved back. I drove over the bumps and through the dust until I reached the Baptist church. Behind the church was the baseball field, a diamond that sparkled in the sun all those summers ago, that summer of youth when we first met.

I pulled off the road onto the gravel lot and slowed to a stop where the gravel met the grass. The church and the grounds were quiet on a Friday morning. I grabbed the shovel and walked through the shade and the shadows of cottonwood trees surrounding the field. Fluffy seeds floated in the air and covered the ground. Patches of grass grew in the outfield, but the infield was all dirt. I nudged the bag at second base with the toe of my shoe and moved it aside. A bit of sand from the torn canvas bag leaked out onto the dust. My spade hit the dirt with a crunch.

A few minutes later, the blade struck a solid object. I dug around the edges and removed more dirt and dropped to my left knee. Moisture from dark soil seeped through the knee of my khakis. My right thigh, bandaged from the bullet that had grazed it, stung a bit. I ignored it. I reached into the hole and pulled out a box and stood up. It might have once been a lunchbox, rusted, dented, and flecked with remnants of red paint. A small brass lock on its side secured a hasp. I found the key on my chain and slid it into the lock. I turned it. The lock fell open.

A folded sheet of paper lay on top of a stack of cash. Other items were beneath the cash, but I didn't want to take an inventory out in the open. I needed to get to my car. I hadn't seen anyone or sensed that I'd been followed, but it paid to be careful. I closed the box and filled the hole and returned to my roadster. A farmer in a truck drove by and slowed down when he saw my car parked in the otherwise empty lot. He moved on, and I drove away from the church until I came to a small creek. A turnoff led to a copse of trees beside the water. I pulled into the shade and cut the engine.

Inside the car, I studied the contents of the box. The folded paper was a letter from Cocky to me dated Sunday, April 17th. That was Easter Sunday. He must have buried the box late that day after church services. The following day we drank beer together in Tom's Inn and listened to the first baseball game of the season. That was the last day I saw Cocky alive. His plane crashed the next morning. The letter began, *Well, Pete, if you're reading this letter I must be dead.*

I read the letter once, then scanned it again, and tucked it into my shirt pocket. Beneath the letter was a stack of cash, bills in various denominations. I counted the larger bills and estimated the count on the smaller ones. It looked to be between thirteen and fourteen thousand dollars. A ledger book with names and notes lay beneath the money along with a number of photographs.

I put everything back in the box. The feds would get the information, but not before I went through it in my office. First I had to take care of the money, and I knew just what to do with it. Cocky died for the information in that box, and I didn't intend to hand it over to the FBI where it would rot in an evidence locker. I rolled back onto the road and drove.

Nothing stirred near the farmhouse when I came over the drive that ran beneath the hedge apple trees. Sundown's pickup truck was parked near the gate. Its door stood open. I cut the engine and listened. Hogs grunted down the lane, and a cardinal chirped in Sissy's elm tree. The dog wasn't lying in her favorite spot in the shade beneath the elm. She didn't greet my arrival with a bark. It seemed too quiet.

I scanned the yard and spotted something brown and white in tall grass beyond the porch. It didn't move. I reached under the dashboard for my Smith and Wesson .38 and slipped it into the pocket of my khakis. When I neared the porch, I saw the dog clearly. Sissy's eyes held an empty stare, her furry coat stained with blood.

I called out Sundown's name, and the screen door slammed against the side of the house. Sundown flew down the steps and ran sobbing into my arms.

"Oh, Pete! They took my babies! They took my Debbie Lynn, and they took my baby Cindy! They shot my Sissy! Oh, my sweet babies, my sweet baby girls."

She sobbed, and I tried to console her.

"Is anyone else in the house?" I said.

Sundown shook her head.

"No! They're gone, gone! I don't know where."

I kept an arm wrapped around Sundown, and we made our way into the house. A teakettle whistled on the stove. Sundown sank into a chair at the kitchen table and held her head in her hands. I took the kettle off the stove. Most of its contents had boiled away. A dry coffeepot with fresh fixings sat nearby.

"What happened, Sundown? Tell me everything," I said.

I refilled the kettle with water and put it back on the stove. She sat up and choked in a breath. She swiped at her eyes with a dishtowel and stared down at the table.

"I don't know what happened. I only just now walked in myself. I came home and saw poor, bloody Sissy. I ran upstairs and yelled for my babies. Nothing but silence. They were gone, no sign of them."

She reared up with wide eyes.

"Maybe the barn. I haven't looked down at the barn, yet," she said. "Maybe they're in the barn. I'll go check the barn."

She grasped at any hope, even hope as wispy as smoke. I held her hands and told her I'd check the barn. I was certain no one was in the barn, but I tried to console her.

"Let's go over everything that happened," I said. "You just got home. Where were you? How long were you gone?"

"I went over to Edna Carmichael's place, a neighbor, to borrow a recipe. That was just over an hour ago, I suppose. I didn't stay long, but Edna insisted I have a cup of coffee. Debbie Lynn was sitting right here at this table when I left, nursing the baby. I got home a few minutes ago and found poor Sissy there in the grass. I knew she was dead as soon as I saw her. I ran into the house and screamed for Debbie and heard nothing but that teakettle whistling. She must have been fixing coffee. What happened, Pete? Tell me what happened. Can you figure it out?"

The kettle whistled again, and I poured the hot water into the coffeepot. I noticed that the water stain on the ceiling had grown.

"Someone kidnapped Debbie Lynn and the baby," I said. "They're alive, Sundown. Whoever took them wants to negotiate, and they need live hostages for leverage. They don't want Debbie Lynn and the baby. They want what Cocky had. They'll need live hostages to get that. They'll contact you soon with their demands, probably by telephone. We have to wait. They came and were gone again within the past hour. That's not long, so they haven't gone far. They'll call when they reach their hideout."

She noticed my bandaged head and brought her hand to her mouth.

"Oh, what happened to you?" she said.

I told her about my accident but spared her the details and assured her I was fine. We waited. I checked the barn and found nothing. I walked around the grounds and came up empty. I wrapped the dog in a blanket and laid her in the shade of the elm tree for later burial. Then, I took the money out of the box in my roadster.

We sat at the table, and Sundown poured coffee. She offered a doughnut, but I declined and lit a cigarette. She broke off a small bit of doughnut with her fingertips and nibbled on it. I reached into my pocket and placed the money on the table. She looked at the money for a long moment and then looked to me for an explanation. I told her I had found Cocky's stash.

"Cocky earned that," I said, "every nickel and more. It belongs to you now."

"Where did the money come from? Is that what they're after?"

I explained that the box held evidence that would incriminate others, and it would clear Cocky at the same time. That evidence was what they were after. The money wouldn't replace Cocky, but it belonged to her now, and no one would come for it. I'd make sure of that. Sundown wanted me to keep some for myself, but I refused.

"You keep it," I said, "all of it."

The phone rang, three short bursts. Sundown shook her head.

"That's Edna's ring," she said.

The party line on the telephone might pose a problem, but there was nothing to be done about that. If the kidnapper called and another party had the line tied up, he'd place his call again. A snoopy neighbor might listen in on the call, but that couldn't be helped either. That was the nature of a party line in rural areas. Families shared a common line, and each party was expected to show courtesy to the others. Each party answered their own ring and no one else's.

An hour went by, then another hour. We smoked cigarettes and sipped coffee. Sundown offered to fix lunch, but I wasn't hungry, and neither was she. By midafternoon, we felt the exhaustion of sitting and waiting. Then the phone rang, two long tones and a short one, and Sundown sat up straight.

"That's me," she said.

We'd gone over the procedure. We stood next to the wall, side-by-side, with the telephone between us. We each had an ear cocked to the receiver. Sundown didn't dawdle over pleasantries.

"Go ahead," she said into the phone.

A voice, male and muffled, came back.

"We've got the girl and the baby. They're unharmed, and they'll stay unharmed if we get what we want. Do you understand?"

"I understand. What do you want?"

"Your husband took something that didn't belong to him. We want it back. If you don't have it, get ahold of that cheap detective your husband palled around with. He broke out of the hospital yesterday. We figure he's hot on the trail of what we're after. Get it. You have until noon tomorrow. If we get what we want before noon, the girl and the baby live."

Earlier, I told Sundown to demand to talk to her daughter. We had to know she was alive.

"Let me speak to Debbie Lynn," she said.

The kidnapper had anticipated the demand, and Debbie Lynn came on the line.

"Momma?"

"Oh, sweetheart, thank God. Are you okay, and Cindy?"

"We're okay, but I'm scared."

"Have they hurt you or touched you?"

She paused.

"No, they haven't hurt me." There was a brief pause, and she spoke again. "I sure could use my Mentholatum."

Sundown raised her eyebrows at me, and the male voice returned.

"That's enough. Now, listen carefully."

He told Sundown she was to place the goods in a brown paper bag and take the bag to the duck pond at Riverside Park in Wichita. There she would find a set of swings in an oak grove that he described. A trash barrel was near the swings. She would place the bag in the barrel. Once he retrieved the package, Debbie Lynn and the baby would be released.

The park was located on a bend of the Little Arkansas River, a popular recreation spot for residents of the city. I wrote the instructions in my book, but I had no intention of following the instructions or meeting his demands. I knew the man who was calling, and I knew where he was calling from. He finished with a warning.

"By noon tomorrow if you want to see your little girls alive."

He disconnected the call.

"What are we going to do?" Sundown said.

"Debbie Lynn is brave," I said. "She's her father's daughter. She sent a signal, just like her dad sent signals to me on the baseball field. She just told us who kidnapped her."

I glanced at the jar of Mentholatum on the table and placed a telephone call to the Hotel Eaton. I asked to speak to a guest, Aaron Bernstein. The shadows outside grew longer. Evening would arrive soon. A voice came over the phone.

"Mr. Bernstein is not in his room, but I think I saw him go into the restaurant earlier. If you'll wait, I'll try to find him."

"Thanks, pal," I said.

A few moments passed, and Bernstein came on the line. I gave him the dope on the kidnapping and told him where the hostages were being held.

"I need your help," I said and added, "They shot the dog."

Bernstein agreed to meet me. I gave him a time and a place, and we hung up the line.

Sundown wiped a dishtowel across her face.

"What do you mean Debbie Lynn sent a signal, Pete? What did she say?"

"She made that comment about her Mentholatum," I said. "That was her signal. She wasn't worried about her chapped lips. She was tipping us to the name of her kidnapper. He's a man employed at Stearman who goes by the name of Chappie."

"Chappie? Who's Chappie? I don't know anyone by that name."

"Your daughter heard Cocky mention his name. She said he didn't care for the man. Debbie Lynn tried to remember the name when I was here before, but she didn't have it right. Not until today that is. She figured I'd be in the picture. She knew I'd visited Stearman to investigate Cocky's death. She threw a signal, and it worked. I've met the man. I know who he is, and I know where he and the girls are now."

24

They shot the dog.

Friday, May 6th

I spotted the silhouette behind the wheel of the dark sedan that was parked in front of the diner on Central. I pulled over to the curb and stopped behind the sedan. Lights shone inside the diner, and a pair of men in dungarees sat at the counter. They looked to be the only customers. I flashed my headlights off and on. I still had my firearm in my pocket. The box of evidence was in the trunk.

Before I left the farm, Sundown hugged me in the shadows.

She said, "Bring them back to me, Pete," and I promised her I would.

Bernstein got out of his sedan and slid onto the front seat of my roadster. I shook his hand and gave him a brief overview of the situation.

"Thanks for this, Bernstein," I said.

He nodded.

"They shot the dog," Bernstein said.

I nodded and pulled away from the curb and drove down Central. I reached the intersection with Sheridan and turned north and rumbled over the railroad tracks, just as I had three nights earlier. I slowed when we reached the house but didn't stop. A light glowed in the kitchen window.

"I was here recently," I said. "Darnell Pettigrew invited me."

"Pettigrew. Is he the guy that did that to your head? You look like you ran into a windmill."

"My scalp's scratched up a bit. His head ended up on a slab."

Even in the dim light, I caught Bernstein's grin. I rolled by the house and explained to Bernstein that the Bund used it for their meetings.

"Pettigrew brought me here for questioning," I said. "He died soon after. The guy inside goes by Chappie. He doesn't know I was here. As far as he knows, this is a safe hideaway for him and his hostages."

At the end of the block I turned around and rolled back. I pulled over and parked at the curb across the street beneath the spreading limbs of a large oak tree. I cut the engine and looked at the sky. The moon had grown in the past few nights.

"Waxing gibbous," I said.

"What's that?" Bernstein said.

"Waxing gibbous, the phase of the moon. The moon's not full, but there's light to see and shadows to hide in. I want to get a look inside that house. I know the layout, but I want to see the girl and the baby."

"Want me to come along?" he said.

"Not yet," I said.

He nodded, and I walked across the street and ducked behind a tree next to the garage. I waited a moment and listened, but I was too far from the house to hear anything. I moved across the driveway and stepped into the shadow of a towering sycamore tree near the corner of the house. The curtains were closed, but a window was raised several inches. A breeze ruffled the curtain. A baby made fussing noises.

"I've got to feed the baby," Debbie Lynn said.

"So, feed the baby," Chappie said.

"Could I have a little privacy please?"

"Stay right where you are. Use this."

Maybe he had a jacket. There wasn't a towel or a blanket in sight the other night.

"How about us? When are we going to eat?" she said. "I can cook, you know, but your icebox is empty. There's nothing to eat in this house."

"Keep your yap shut. Everything's Jake. Food is on the way. Keep quiet until it gets here."

I heard no other voices, so I ducked through the shadows and returned to the car.

"I couldn't see, but I heard them talking inside. It's Chappie all right. They're in the kitchen. They're waiting for food, so someone else is coming."

"Food?" Bernstein said.

"Yeah. Chappie is a loose cannon. I figure he's making it up as he goes. I doubt if he planned this kidnapping. I figure he went to the farm to brace Sundown. When she didn't show, he grabbed the girl and the baby and hightailed it. They're waiting for a delivery. That means an accomplice. Whoever delivers the food will be our ticket into the house. Let's go back and wait."

We moved through the shadows. Bernstein took a position next to the garage, and I hid near the porch beneath the sycamore tree. It may have been ten or twenty minutes, but it seemed like an hour. A pickup truck chugged down the street, bounced into the gravel driveway, and came to a stop. Fingers pulled the kitchen curtain back an inch or so, then the curtain fell back into place. A figure climbed out of the cab of the truck, a mountain of flesh dressed in bib overalls and an undershirt. He reached back into the cab and pulled out a box. The hinges on the door groaned when he bumped it shut with his broad backside.

Bernstein came out of the shadows, stepped behind the figure, and jammed a pistol into his spine. The guy's mouth fell open, and he almost dropped the box he carried. I caught it and put it back in his hands.

"Keep your mouth shut, Orsulak," I said. "Not a peep until I say so."

He nodded.

"Get Chappie to open the door," I whispered.

Orsulak lumbered onto the porch and kicked the door with the toe of his boot.

"It's open," Chappie said through the door.

Orsulak looked at me, and I shook my head.

"Open the door," he said. "My hands are full."

"You helpless tub of lard," Chappie said.

The door swung open, and I body blocked Orsulak aside. He yelped and went off the porch along with the box of groceries. The sound of breaking glass followed his scream. Chappie looked puzzled and tried to slam the door shut. He failed. I caught the door with my hip and poked the business end of my .38 under his chin. In a low voice I begged him to do something stupid. Part of me wished he would.

Debbie Lynn stood up from the table with the baby in her arms and screamed my name. From over my shoulder, I heard the strike of a match and smelled the pleasant aroma of burning tobacco.

"Nice work, sleuth, but you cow town boys are no fun," Bernstein said.

He leapt onto the porch and threw a punch that caught Chappie in the midsection just below the sternum. Chappie was no lightweight, but he huffed and doubled over with a groan. He gagged, and greasy bile spilled over his lips and dripped onto the porch. Bernstein stepped back and admired his work. Not a crease on his suit was mussed. The man never even lost the ash on his cigar.

"That's for shooting the dog," he said.

Orsulak sat up in the driveway and wheezed.

"Keep an eye on this one," I said.

Bernstein leveled his gun at Chappie and grinned like a wolf standing over a lamb. Chappie froze. I stepped down off the porch and leaned over Orsulak. Bits of gravel clung to his overalls, and he sweated like racehorse. Even in the moonlight I could see he looked bad. He wheezed and struggled to breathe. He held his hands over his chest.

"The doctor!" he said, "The doctor!"

"I'll call an ambulance," I said. "Hang on."

He shook his head.

"No. No ambulance! The doctor! The doctor!"

"I'll get you a doctor," I said. "Sit still."

He shook his head again.

"No. Listen! The doctor!"

He stiffened and went quiet. He clutched his chest. His eyes rolled back, and I saw their whites. He fell backwards onto the driveway and didn't move. He didn't wheeze. He didn't breathe. It was too late for the doctor. Sam Orsulak was dead.

I made calls from the telephone in the house, first to the police and then to Sundown. I let Debbie Lynn tell her Mom that she was safe and would be home soon. The police arrived and carted Chappie off to jail. They wanted Debbie Lynn to make a statement, but I protested. The hour was late, and I had to get her and the baby home to Sundown. The statement could wait. I promised to visit the station myself. An ambulance arrived and hauled Orsulak's remains to the morgue. The cops helped the medics lift the body onto a stretcher. I drove Bernstein back to his car and thanked him for his help.

"My pleasure," he said. "That's the most fun I've had since I hit this town."

By the time we got to the farm, the night was nearly spent, and so was I. The women hugged and cried. I left them in the kitchen and found my way back to my place on Lewellen. The last thing I remembered was dropping into bed. I was asleep when my bandaged head hit the pillow.

25

We'll get him.

Monday, May 9th

The weekend came and went. I sailed through it like a ship in the fog, not dead in the water but adrift and rudderless. I didn't leave the house. I slept when I got tired, and I ate when I got hungry. I slept long hours, and I didn't shave or bathe. The more I slept, the worse I looked, but the better I felt. I listened to the clocks and paid no attention to the time. On Saturday, I ate like a child and drank like a sailor. My diet featured peanut butter and bourbon.

I turned on the radio. Somber organ music played, and a deep, haunting voice spoke. "Who knows what evil lurks in the hearts of men? The Shadow knows!" Then came sneering laughter. I listened to the mystery show and slouched in my chair and came awake at midnight. My glass that had held bourbon was empty. I brewed a pot of coffee and smoked cigarettes till dawn. Then I went to bed and slept all day Sunday.

On Monday morning, I sat behind my desk and pored over the contents of the box. I had bathed and shaved and donned a pressed suit. I wouldn't be invited to grace the cover of a fashion magazine, but Agnes didn't gasp when I arrived at the office, either. She smiled and handed me a cup of coffee. Then she kissed her finger and pressed it to the tip of my nose.

"Welcome back," she said.

I read Cocky's letter, then I went through the box. After that, I read Cocky's letter again.

Well, Pete, if you're reading this letter I must be dead.

Yes, Cocky was dead, along with the pilot who flew his plane. Senseless deaths. Someone ordered their deaths. Someone else followed those orders and carried out the executions. The crash was no accident.

Darnell Pettigrew is my boss. Start there. He tried to recruit me into an organization, the German American Bund. They're bad people, Pete. I went to some of their meetings and told Pettigrew I wanted nothing to do with them. We had a falling out. I kept an eye on him and caught him taking pictures, the guts inside one of our planes. Some of those pictures are in the box. I tried to tell Mr. Veatch, but Pettigrew framed me, said I took the pictures. I found these in Pettigrew's stuff, along with the book and the pile of money. I grabbed it all. Now he's after me. He's selling secrets. To who I don't know.

Darnell Pettigrew was dead. He died, and his secrets died with him. I looked at the photographs. The ones of the aircraft meant little to me. Gordon Veatch at Stearman would evaluate them. Other photographs were taken inside the meeting house. One showed a speaker in the living room addressing men who sat in chairs. The speaker stood between two flags. One flag was the stars and stripes, the other a Nazi swastika. The speaker was Martin Richter.

There's someone else, too, a guy who came over from Boeing to look at our planes. I thought I didn't know him. Then I heard him speak. It was Sam Orsulak. I didn't recognize him. He's put on weight. I don't trust him. You know why.

Sam Orsulak lost Cocky's trust the day he backed away from that fly ball. Orsulak was dead, too. What secrets went with him?

I studied the ledger book. Dates and names were entered in pencil and ran down the left-hand column. Most of the names were listed several times. Were they Bund members? Stearman employees? Both? Dollar figures followed each name, posted in the next column. Did the figures signify money paid out in exchange for trade secrets? If so, who financed the operation? Where did the money come from?

Toward the back of the ledger more dollar figures were posted, larger amounts in round figures. There were no names listed with the money, but at the top of the page the word Mister was followed by a dash: Mister –. Was Mister Dash the source of the money?

I left the ledger book with Agnes along with instructions to type everything on its pages in duplicate. I left the pictures in the box, and locked the box in my desk. I carried Cocky's letter in my pocket.

The needle on the gasoline tank hovered above the E. I turned south on St. Francis and pulled into a Golden Rule filling station. A young man in a khaki uniform and bow tie grinned and went to work. He filled the tank, washed the windshield, and checked the oil. He measured the pressure on the tires, chatted about the weather and baseball, and never lost his grin. The station's founder, Elbert Rule, instilled the Golden Rule philosophy in his workers. The young man did unto his customers as he would have them do unto him.

"That'll be ninety cents," he said when he finished.

I handed him a buck and returned the grin. It was contagious.

"Keep the change," I said.

I drove west on William and pulled up at the police station. The uniformed cops who had arrested Chappie Friday night were off duty, so I left my statement with a sergeant. I gave him Debbie Lynn's full name and told him how to reach her.

"We have this Chappie character behind bars," he said. "His name is Wade Chapman. A pair of federal agents in black suits interrogated him this morning."

I nodded and said I'd met them. McCormick strolled by the desk.

"Are you back here already?" he said. "What now?"

I told him about the kidnapping.

"Stone, you manage to find more trouble than any other citizen in the city," he said.

I wasn't in the mood for Mac's gibes.

"Those are mean streets out there in the city. If the cops did better work, those citizens would be safer."

"Don't talk to me about doing better work. Talk to your barber."

When I left the police station, the grin I'd picked up at the filling station had gone. I found a beanery on First Street and ordered a ham sandwich and coffee. I opened my notebook to a fresh page and wrote the word Mister followed by a dash. I added mustard to the sandwich and chewed a bite.

Pettigrew, who was no sage, used the coded name. Mister Dash could have been anyone in the Bund, but it had to be someone with the dough to finance an espionage operation. The money to pay off the underlings who took the pictures may have come from out of town. Or, maybe someone with money in Wichita bought the pictures and brokered them to buyers from out of town. A guy could buy the pictures and sell them to someone else, someone connected to a national organization like the German American Bund. It would have to be a guy with lots of dough and few scruples, a guy like Martin Richter.

I wrote down Mister.

Then I wrote Mr.

Then I wrote M.R.

Then I wrote Martin Richter.

When I returned to the office, Agnes had completed her task. She handed me three typewritten pages. I folded them and tucked them into my jacket pocket.

"Thanks, kiddo," I said.

"What about the carbons?"

"File them in the cabinet."

I retrieved the box from my desk and added the ledger to it. I tucked the box under an arm and winked at Agnes when I left the office. I drove south on Oliver and recalled Friday night's drive on Broadway, the street that ran parallel a number of blocks to the west. When I reached the intersections at Kellogg, Lincoln, Harry, and all the other cross streets, I slowed down and obeyed the signals like a good citizen.

I arrived at the Stearman offices, parked the roadster, and went inside. Mrs. Richeson had the telephone to her ear. When she spotted me, she spoke quickly into the receiver and hung up.

"He left orders not to be disturbed," she said. "Don't you ever make an appointment?"

I removed my fedora, and she saw my bandaged head.

"Oh, dear," she said. "Are you all right?"

"Why Mrs. Richeson," I said. "I never knew you cared. Call the boys in black."

I knocked once on Gordon Veatch's door and went in. Veatch hunched over a blueprint on his drafting table, shirtsleeves rolled to the elbows and a cigar stub in his mouth.

"I didn't expect to see you today," he said. "Aren't you supposed to be taking it easy?"

"We don't have much time," I said.

He moved to his desk, and I took a chair across from him.

"The federal boys are on the way. I recovered this."

I opened the box and removed the ledger and photographs. Veatch glanced through the pictures and let out a low whistle. He opened the ledger and scanned the names.

"Damn it," he said. "I know some of these men. This is disappointing. I'd like to have Mrs. Richeson make a copy."

"I've got a copy right here," I said and handed him the pages Agnes had typed.

Veatch raised his eyebrows.

"You've been busy," he said.

He looked through the photographs again. Agents Young and Townsend arrived. We all moved to the conference table. I lit a cigarette while Veatch went through the photographs with the agents and explained what they were. They thumbed through the ledger, and Young stuck it into his pocket.

"I'd tell you that you'll get a copy of this," he said to Veatch, "but I doubt that is necessary. I suppose you already have a copy."

He paused for a reply, and when he didn't get one, he turned to me.

"Okay, Stone, let's have it. Where did you find this information?"

"It came from Cocky Wright, my deceased pal and a standup American. He left it in a place where only I would find it."

I gave them the story, how Cocky had discovered that Pettigrew had taken the photographs, and how he learned that others were in on it, too. I told them about the German American Bund, their meetings in the house on Sheridan, and I pointed to the photographs on the table.

"He tried to warn his superiors, but his boss was one of the culprits. When Cocky blew the whistle, someone rigged the plane to crash, probably Pettigrew or Orsulak. They wanted him gone. Someone also planted evidence in Cocky's toolbox to incriminate him."

The feds would keep everything, of course, but I wanted to convince Veatch that Stearman Aircraft had been compromised, and I wanted to clear Cocky Wright's name. The feds had the written record Pettigrew kept that included the names of men who worked at Stearman and others at Boeing. If the men also belonged to the Bund, that wasn't illegal, but espionage was, and the men listed would be investigated.

"We talked to Chapman this morning," Young said.

I nodded and told him I'd just left the police station myself.

"Once Pettigrew was out of the picture, Chapman tried to horn in on his scam," Young said. "He didn't realize what he was getting into. Orsulak approached him with the idea that there was money to be made. Chapman went along with Orsulak and got in over his head. Before Chapman got involved, Pettigrew and

Orsulak worked together. Pettigrew called the shots. It was Pettigrew and Orsulak who broke into your house. They were convinced from the beginning that you had the dope Wright left behind."

"Which one rigged that plane to crash?" I said.

"Does it matter?" he said. "I'd finger Orsulak for that. He inspected the planes. He had the knowledge, and he had the opportunity. He followed orders. What else have you got Stone? What haven't you told us?"

I could have lied and said they had everything, but I didn't. There was more, and I didn't care if they knew it.

"Cocky left me a letter. It's personal, and you can't have it. The only names he mentioned belong to the deceased, Pettigrew and Orsulak. Everything else he wrote in the letter concerns the items on the table along with personal remarks addressed to me."

Young thought that over. He could order me to hand over the letter. He didn't.

"Anything else?" he said.

"Yes. There was some dough, a pile of it. You can't have that either."

Agent Townsend couldn't resist. He had to chime in.

"I knew it," he said. "When it comes down to it, you're just a cheap gumshoe in it for the dough."

Agent Young shot him a look, and Townsend curbed his tongue.

"The money is evidence," Young said.

"Exactly," I said. "Evidence and nothing more. Maybe the money came from Richter. Maybe it came from someone we don't know. Maybe Pettigrew stole it. It doesn't matter. My pal ended up dead. He earned that money."

Young nodded and looked thoughtful.

"I'm satisfied. I suspect a widow lady will be putting a new roof on her house soon," he said.

Young was satisfied, but I wasn't, and it showed. I still had questions. Uncertainties gnawed at me. Veatch held a match to the stub in his mouth.

"You did good work, Stone, uncovering this material," Veatch said. "You should be pleased."

"That's right," Young said.

"I'm not pleased. Several people are dead. The snake is dead, but the head survives. The head will grow a new tail. Maybe Orsulak did rig the plane to crash. He didn't do it on his own. Someone gave the order. You said it yourself. I think I know who it was, but I can't prove it."

I had Young open the ledger to the pages at the back, and I shared my suspicions regarding the identity of Mister Dash.

"I can't prove Martin Richter is financing an espionage scam, but all the evidence points to him," I said. "If anyone is giving orders, it must be him. That's his picture on the table, but what does that picture prove? It just shows a politician talking to an organization of men. Maybe Mister Dash is someone else."

Young thought that over.

"I wouldn't worry, Stone. I think you're right about Richter. I think we'll prove it."

"How?"

Young considered my question for a long moment before he spoke.

"The pipeline to the top no longer exists. In your words, the snake is dead. No matter. The head still needs to be fed. If the head is Richter, we'll find out."

I raised my eyebrows, and he tapped his forefinger on the ledger.

"Maybe one of the men listed here will feed the head. Maybe a man on this list will take over Pettigrew's operation. Maybe a man on this list is an operative for the FBI. Don't worry, Stone. We'll get him."

26

Her name meant sorrows.

Thursday, May 19th

It unfolded just as Agent Young promised it would. The papers covered the story, both *The Eagle* and *The Beacon*. They didn't have all the facts, the papers seldom did, but what they did report was accurate if not complete. A budding young political candidate was caught up in an espionage scandal. Martin Richter, candidate for Congress, was accused of purchasing sensitive information on military aircraft from Stearman Aircraft Company and from Boeing Aircraft Company. When a Stearman employee attempted to sell secret plans to Richter, federal agents moved in and arrested the pair. The papers went on to say that information obtained by the FBI from an anonymous source named other employees involved in an espionage ring, and the investigation was ongoing.

The papers didn't mention that the Stearman employee caught with Richter was a federal agent and the entire sting operation was staged by the FBI. No matter. The district attorney would take over, and the courts would decide Richter's fate. His political career was over. His marriage would end, too. What was the cost of a man's life? Money, it was always the money. Richter once said he grew up on beans and cornbread. I doubted if a menu in prison would be any better.

I took a five spot out of my wallet and laid it on my desk. I tried to look old Abe in the eyes, but the stony character wouldn't return my gaze. He looked to the side, past my shoulder like I wasn't even there. Silver certificate. The United States of America. Payable to the Bearer on Demand. The money, always the money.

I thought about Sam Orsulak, that poor slob who sold out his team for a lousy twenty dollar bill. Even Judas held out for thirty pieces of silver. The money, always the money. Sam ended up dead, clutching at his chest, and calling for the doctor. The doctor.

I picked up the telephone and placed a call. The operator connected me to a number in Kansas City, a private detective I'd known for years. When he came on the phone, we reminisced for a moment, then I asked him some questions. I hoped he'd do some research for me and get back to me with what he found.

"There's no need for research," he said. "I know the story. Everyone around here knows the story."

So, he talked, and I listened. Twenty minutes later, I thanked him and hung up the phone. I lit a cigarette and stared at Abe. He still looked past me. When I finished the cigarette, I crushed the butt in the ashtray and returned the five spot to my wallet. Then I went for a drive.

The sign in front of the house read "For Sale." I followed the winding driveway through the manicured lawn and pulled up at the pebbled walkway. I cut the engine on the roadster. When I pushed the button on the door, the chimes bonged with a hollow sound. Several moments passed before the door opened. Even with her disheveled auburn curls, the woman looked stunning.

"It's you," she said. "Why am I not surprised to see you?"

Her syllables were not as crisp as they might have been. The lady had been drinking. The booze slurred her speech, but it didn't dull those ice blue eyes. Her cold stare cut like a razor. She wore a dark blue dress that matched her eyes and clung to the right places. She wore no shoes. She turned on a bare heel and walked away. The door remained open. I went inside and closed the door behind me.

She entered the study with its desk, sofa, and wingback chairs in French provincial design, the room where I'd once waited for her husband, Martin Richter. The curtains were drawn, and the lights were turned off. The study was lit by a glow from the fireplace that cast shadows on the walls. A pair of black, high-heeled shoes lay tipped over and abandoned in the middle of the Persian rug. The Robert Henri painting of the young girl in red curls hung on the wall behind the desk. The fire kept the room as toasty as the sunny day outside.

The charred remains of papers, documents, and photographs smoldered in the flames. Delores Richter dropped into the chair behind the desk with an inelegant plop. She poured Boodles gin straight from the bottle into a crystal tumbler and drank it neat, no ice and no mixer. A cigarette burned in an ashtray.

"Join me?" she said.

"No, thanks. So, you're here all alone? No more Maynard?"

"Alas, dear Maynard has departed. Moved on to greener pastures. The rats have abandoned the sinking ship. Yes, I am alone, thanks to you, Pete Stone, and your cheap detective skills. Yes, I'm alone."

I looked at the painting on the wall behind Delores. The young girl with the long red curls and ice blue eyes stared back. Delores followed my gaze.

"I was barely a teenager then. Father commissioned Robert Henri to paint that. My father knew Henri years ago when they were boys, growing up in Nebraska. His name was Cozad then. He's dead now."

"Yes, I know," I said and lit a cigarette. "Robert Henri is dead. So is your father."

She raised her eyebrows and poured Boodles into her glass. She poured more of the gin into a second glass.

"Drink with me," she said. "I hate to drink alone."

I reached for the glass and took a sip.

"You haven't been honest with me," I said. "You told me your father was a wealthy man. You led me to believe he was alive and well in Kansas City."

The fire crackled. Delores reached into a desk drawer and retrieved a stack of papers. She pushed herself up with both hands on the arms of her chair. She stepped slowly to the fireplace and fed papers into the blaze. Then, she returned to her chair and plopped down again.

"I didn't lie to you. My father was a wealthy man. He was alive and well and living in Kansas City, just as I told you. We had a wonderful life together, my father and I. He was a king, and I was his princess. He used to take me to the park to ride the carousel when I was a little girl. They even had a miniature train that went through the park. We ate ice cream, strawberry cones with sprinkles. I suppose he was the only man I ever really loved."

She gazed into the fire when she spoke.

"That was before," she said.

"Before your father got greedy?"

Her head snapped back toward me.

"What do you know?" she said. "What do you know about anything, you lousy bum? Greedy? My father was the most generous man in the world. He was never greedy. You think you know a lot. You don't know a thing about my father, what he went through."

"Your father was a businessman. He invested in the stock market, leveraged his holdings. He lost his fortune speculating in the stock market. He wasn't alone. A lot of other smart men did the same thing."

She reached into a purse on her desk and pulled out a cigarette. I leaned across the desk and lit it for her.

"My father didn't speculate. It wasn't greed that ruined him."

She paused and drew several puffs from her cigarette. She tipped her glass and swallowed.

"Mother got sick. She was dying, cancer of the pancreas. Her doctors were helpless. They told my father there was nothing they could do. Keep her comfortable, they said. They fed her pills, pain pills mostly, and left her to wither away. My father couldn't accept that. He didn't make a fortune by sitting idly while fate turned the screw. He was a man of action."

She crushed out her cigarette and poured gin into her glass. She held the bottle toward me and raised her eyebrows, but I shook my head.

"When my father learned about a treatment in Switzerland, he grasped a glimmer of hope. It was experimental, but at least the doctors there would do something. They flew to Switzerland, my father and mother along with a nurse. He chartered a plane so mother could fly lying down in a bed.

"Father left me at boarding school to be looked after by the headmistress. He left his money in a bank to be managed. It was managed, all right, by a conniving Jew. This was nine years ago. Everything went fine at first. School started, and I kept busy. I missed my parents, but I'd outgrown carousels and sprinkles. Then came October, Black Tuesday, and you know what happened. The stock market crashed. The Jew lost all of my father's money. Father returned home that Christmas with mother's body in a coffin. His wife was dead, and his fortune was gone, evaporated into thin air. The bank, the Jew, and the money all disappeared along with the woman he loved. It broke my father, financially and mentally. He never recovered."

She stopped and stared into the fire for a moment. Then she spoke.

"Father didn't die right away. We managed together on the money in my trust. It survived the crash. It was nothing like his wealth, but at least we had something to live on. Then Martin came along. I was young and vulnerable, eager to start a fresh life. Father tried to stop me. He saw through Martin. Father had already lost a wife, and he was afraid of losing me, too. Afraid of being alone, I suppose. I didn't listen. I thought I loved Martin, and we ran off together and got married. Father died not long after."

I left unspoken a detail that we both knew. Delores's father had committed suicide, leaving a gun next to his body and a note on a table. She poured Boodles into her glass, then she poured some into mine.

"Is that how we got here?" I said. "Is that why my friend died along with the others? Has your husband's espionage scheme and his association with the German American Bund been nothing but a twisted plot of revenge? You blame a Jewish banker for your father's failure, so you lash out at all Jews, people you hold responsible for your father's bankruptcy. Is that it?"

"The German American Bund will save America from itself," she said, "by ridding the country of Jews. I believe that and so do many others."

"And your husband believes that? Is that why he's under arrest?"

"My husband believes what he's told to believe. Stupid Martin. Martin was careless, careless and foolish."

"How many people have to die to balance the scales?" I said. "Your husband's life is in ruins. My friend and his pilot are dead. Pettigrew and Orsulak are dead. Orsulak died of heart failure, screaming for the doctor. I thought he cried out for medical attention, but he didn't. He knew it was too late for that. He cried out to warn me. Doctor or Dr., spelled with a D and an R. Another stupid code name like Mister, M and R for Martin Richter. The letters D and R stand for Delores Richter. You're the doctor. Orsulak tried to tell me it was you."

"Sam Orsulak was another fool," she said.

"Did Orsulak rig that plane to crash? Did you order him to do it?"

"Sam Orsulak did what he had to do. No, I didn't order him to rig that plane as you put it. My order was simple. Either recover whatever Wright stole from us or take care of Wright and make sure the information he had was buried with him. How Sam Orsulak got that done was of no interest to me."

There was the answer I'd been searching for. Sam Orsulak killed Cocky Wright and the pilot. Delores Richter pushed the button and gave the order. Do what needed to be done. I had a bad taste in my mouth, and it wasn't from the Boodles.

"You say your husband is careless and foolish, but you stayed with him. You used him. You didn't love him, and he didn't love you. You were nothing but his meal ticket. Why didn't you leave him?"

She didn't reply. She looked at me and sipped her gin. Her blue eyes didn't waver. The answer dawned on me, the answer to my own question.

"So, that's it. You weren't Martin's meal ticket. Martin was your meal ticket."

"The man is devoid of character, incapable of love and affection, but he's the perfect politician. Hand him a microphone and put him in front of an audience, and he turns into a magician. He has a knack for knowing what his audience wants to hear, so he tells them what they want to hear. They listen. They write checks to support their candidate. Bingo, gumshoe.

"I didn't lose the money in my trust when the market collapsed, but we squandered it these past years pandering to a lavish lifestyle. Martin never worried, though. Martin had a plan. A politician with no scruples can make a lot of money. Smart men, wealthy men, entranced by Martin's blather, open their wallets and checkbooks, eager to buy what he sells, currying his favor, and willing to pay for the privilege."

"I've seen him at work," I said.

"The Bund approached Martin early on. They recognized his talents. First they sponsored his candidacy. Later, they suggested he use his talents to get information on the aircraft industry. I don't blame Martin entirely for what has happened. I encouraged him. We didn't have a perfect marriage, but we had a marriage of the minds."

"You needed money, so you did what you did, and people died," I said.

"You say the word money like it's a bitter herb. It's one thing to outgrow carousels and sprinkles. It's quite another to be unable to afford them. No one wanted your friend to die. Pettigrew and Orsulak tried to buy your friend's information, but he wouldn't listen. He was just like you, too good to take our money. Your friend was stubborn. It cost him his life."

She poured gin into both glasses. I pushed my glass away.

"I'm through drinking with you lady. Your booze tastes lousy, and you stink."

She acted as if she hadn't heard my comment. She reached into her purse again. Instead of a cigarette, she pulled out a gun, a chrome plated derringer, and leveled it at my torso.

"Yeah, I stink," she said. "The whole rotten world stinks."

"Killing me will make everything right, is that it?"

"Killing you would be easy, but it wouldn't change a thing. Martin would still be in jail, and I'd still be headed to the poor house. Father was a man of action. He taught me well. I'll do what I have to do. I told you before, I'm my father's daughter."

She raised the derringer and cocked the hammer. I cried out, "No!" and leapt forward, but it was too late. The blast echoed off the shadowed walls. The bullet traveled through the roof of her mouth and exited the back of her skull. I went rigid on the desk, propped on all fours, frozen by the sound of the gunfire and the sight of blood and brains that stained the wall behind her. The young girl in the red curls stared at me from her framed perch on the wall. Her blue eyes didn't blink. A single, scarlet tear slid down her cheek.

Delores Richter, the woman whose name meant sorrows, lay sprawled in the chair. Blood leaked from her auburn curls and dripped onto the Persian rug. Her ice blue eyes didn't blink either. They stared at nothing at all.

27

You got moxie.

Friday, May 20th

I spent much of the morning at the farm with Sundown and Debbie Lynn. When I drove in, I noticed a fresh mound of earth beneath the branches of the elm tree. A small cross was planted atop the mound. Roofing shingles were stacked on a pallet near the end of the house.

The three of us sat at the kitchen table and drank coffee. The baby slept in another room. I did most of the talking. A telephone call would have been easier, but Sundown and Debbie Lynn deserved to hear the story from me in person. Also, a call would have tied up the party line and lured uninvited ears into the conversation. They listened without interruption until I was finished speaking. The puzzle became clear, and even though the puzzle was ugly, all of the pieces fit together. If the narration didn't bring peace, it at least brought a sense of finality and relief to them and to me.

Later, back in my office, I sat at my desk and pulled Cocky's letter out of my pocket. I read through it and reached the final lines.

Do what has to be done, Pete. I know you can do it. And when you've finished, I know you'll look after my girls. I don't have to ask. You got moxie, kid.

Agnes knocked and opened the door.

"You have company," she said.

Three men walked into my office, two in matching dark suits, and the third a dapper dresser decked out in tailored, pinstripe threads. A diamond ring flashed on his pinkie finger.

"Well, if it isn't gold, frankincense, and myrrh," I said.

"Always the wise guy," FBI Agent Townsend said.

"Was that a reference to the Christ child?" Bernstein asked.

"That was a comment on your wisdom," I said.

Bernstein grinned and lit a cigar.

"To what do I owe the visit?" I said.

"We came by to say so long," Agent Young said. "We didn't get off on the right foot, but you turned out to be a square shooter, Stone. Your methods aren't textbook, but your results are commendable. You helped us out, and we're grateful."

"I hope we accomplished something," I said. "My friend and several others are dead. Was it worth it?"

"We broke up a ring of criminals that attempted to sell secrets that could have threatened the country. They've been stopped. That's a good thing."

"I hope so. I hope Cocky didn't die in vain."

"Don't be too hard on your pal," Young said, "and don't be too hard on yourself. We didn't break up the Bund, but we kicked them in the shins, and we'll keep kicking them in the shins. Your friend won't be forgotten, not by those who matter. He uncovered key information, and you deserve our thanks for bringing it to us."

We talked for several minutes, and they put on their hats and started to leave.

"Wait a minute, fellas," I said. "There's something I've neglected to do."

I reached into a desk drawer and pulled out a bottle.

"One evening you came into my office and rummaged through my desk. I made a crack about this bottle of rye. I said someday we'd drink it together. Gentlemen, this is the day."

Agnes heard me through the open door and brought glasses

into my office. I cracked the seal on the bottle and poured. We raised our glasses.

"This is for Archibald 'Cocky' Wright, a brave American and a good friend, who once tossed a kid worn out piece of leather and showed him how to play the game."

"Here, here," Young said.

We tossed back our drinks. Young offered his hand, and I shook it. Then, I shook Bernstein's hand and Townsend's, too. We said our goodbyes, and they left. Agnes closed the door behind her when she left.

I stood alone in my office and gazed out the window, looking west down Douglas Avenue. I spotted the Allis Hotel and the Fourth National Bank and other buildings I drove past each day. I thought I might give Lucille a call and take her to dinner. How would we celebrate, I wondered? Steaks? Barbeque?

I couldn't see it, but Lawrence Stadium sat beyond downtown, an alabaster jewel on the west bank of the Arkansas River, glistening in the sun with her red, white, and blue pennants waving in the breeze.

We'd celebrate with a hot dog, I thought. A hot dog was the perfect food for our celebration, a hot dog served the way it was meant to be served, with mustard, beer, and baseball. Yes, baseball. There would be a game at Lawrence Stadium later that day. There would be baseball. There would always be baseball.

The End

Dear Reader,

The characters and stories in the *Shadow* series are fictional, but I hope to make the reader's journey through 1930s Wichita as realistic as possible. Pete Stone is a figment of my imagination, but he is inspired by memories of my grandfather, Pete Graves, who lived in and around Wichita during this era. An address on Lewellen taken from my birth certificate was once home to Grandpa. He lived there along with an extensive collection of clocks that Pete Stone inherited.

The characters in Pete's stories are fictional with the exception of brief references to historical figures. Characters that play key roles in Pete's stories, such as Martin and Delores Richter in this book, are fictional, but Fritz Kuhn did lead the German American Bund until he was convicted of embezzlement and deported. Robert Henri (he pronounced it Hen Rye) lived in Cozad, Nebraska as a boy and was a noted artist prior to the events in this story. Pete's roadster was built by the Jones Motor Car Company that existed in Wichita from about 1914 to 1921. Stearman Aircraft was founded in 1927 and became a part of Boeing Corporation in 1938, although the characters and events regarding Stearman in Pete's stories are all fictional.

Details such as prices of food, clothing, and gasoline represent the era. The movies at the local theaters and the baseball games on the radio are based on factual reports. Much of my information comes from reading microfilm copies of Wichita newspapers and from reading books and researching websites pertinent to the time and place.

I strive to make the experience realistic, but the stories are lies and whoppers born from my imagination. Nevertheless, ten thousand fans did watch Jim Bagby of the Boston Red Sox beat Red Ruffing of the New York Yankees by a score of eight to four on a drizzly opening day in 1938. As Casey Stengel, the long ago manager of the Yankees was fond of saying, "You could look it up."

Thanks for joining Pete Stone on his latest adventure. Both he and I appreciate you.

Mike Graves

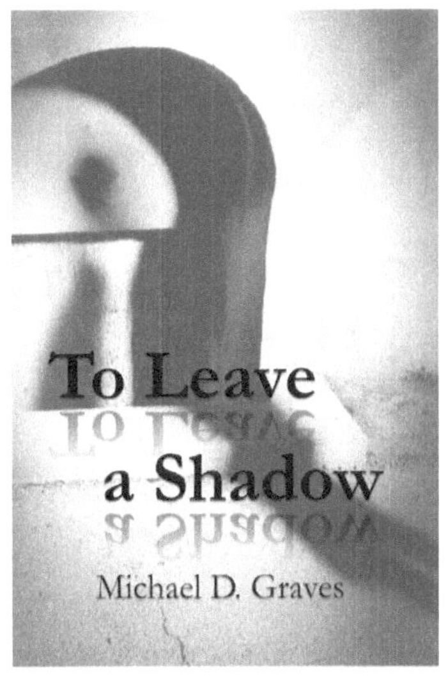

Publisher: Meadowlark - 2015
ISBN: 978-0692567791

Spring 1937

Black flies swarmed over the body, even before they got it out of the water. The buzzing, hissing swirl made a difficult job even harder. Two cops, one on each side of the bloated corpse, grunted and swore as they struggled against the river current. Each grabbed a hold under a limp arm and tugged against the powerful eddies, leaning backwards to gain leverage, fighting for purchase on the river bottom. The muddy water flowed over and around the soggy mass. They gasped for air and gagged when they sucked it in. The stench was thick and foul, the sort that lingers in your nostrils and wakes you late at night and puts you off your breakfast the next morning.

I smoked a cigarette and watched the struggle. It was humid, and I was perspiring. I took off my hat and wiped my brow with a handkerchief. My shirt stuck to my back. Rivulets of sweat trickled down my neck. I stuck a finger inside my collar and raised my head to take in some fresh air, but it was fruitless. To the south, a meat packing plant belched out rancid offal fumes. To the west, a bakery added a sticky, sweet cinnamon scent. The odors from the factories mingled beneath the heavy clouds and descended on the city below. It smelled like a fart in a pastry shop.

Somewhere in the distance a horn honked and then another. A church bell rang and tires rumbled over brick streets. Brakes squealed. A siren wailed in the distance and a plane flew overhead.

Several people stood around the perimeter, shifting from foot to foot, gawking and then looking away in disgust. Almost any-place else in the city would have been more pleasant, but our species has an innate urge to observe the grotesque. Some watched, others covered their mouths or mumbled to companions, and someone bent over and gagged. Somebody swore softly, and somebody coughed.

The two policemen finally dragged the body ashore, and the buzz of the flies grew louder. The uniformed cops bent over at the waist with their hands on their knees gasping for air. I stared down at the swollen corpse and swallowed the bile rising in my throat. I thought about the poor bastard who once inhabited that body and pondered the fickleness of fate. Why him? What had he ever done? Why not him? Does anyone deserve to die like this?

I thought about his widow sitting at home, eager for him to return, and I wondered how she would react when she got the gruesome news. How else could she react? She'd crumble like a KO'd boxer. This guy wouldn't be coming home tonight or any other night. He'd never again come through the door, peck his wife on the cheek, and ask what's for dinner. She'd never again ask him about his day. His life was over, spent, wrung out of him by a muddy, roiling river. Life is fragile, life is futile, and we all cash in one way or another, but this guy had drawn a particularly lousy death. I looked down at the rotting mass and crushed my cigarette beneath my shoe. I continued to stare at the body for a long moment. I shook my head and asked myself for maybe the hundredth time why I'd ever gotten into this business.

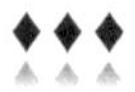

Publisher: Meadowlark - 2017
ISBN: 978-0-9966801-6-5

Saturday, June 5

The first time I met the cop we had words. You might've called it an altercation. Maybe even a fight. It was night, late at night, going into the wee hours of the morning, and I'd been drinking, again. I'd been drinking a lot lately. The cop braced me on the sidewalk down the street from Tom's Inn, planting a fleshy paw on my chest with a stiff arm. He flashed a grin that bore not a trace of good humor. He leaned in and sniffed my breath and snapped his head back.

"Ugh, man. You smell like a drunken bum. You're stink-o, you are. Who are you, buddy? What's your name?"

I fumbled through my pockets and pulled out a card.

"Pete Stone, Private Investigations," he said. "So, you're a gumshoe. Well, you're drunk, gumshoe. I hope you don't think you're going to drive your fancy automobile over my city streets in your condition. Cause if you do, you've got another think coming."

I stood under a yellow streetlight. My Jones Six Roadster, top down, was parked at the curb three steps away. My keys dangled from my fingertips. I glanced at my car. I glanced at my keys. I looked at the cop.

"Wise deduction, Sherlock," I said. I may have slurred. "How'd you figure that?"

Tom and I had spent the better part of the evening perched on barstools, swapping stories and lies, and lowering the level of a bottle of rye whiskey. We'd discussed our lives, what we'd done, what we hadn't done, what we wished we hadn't done. We'd bounced around the country's problems and agreed the solution to halting the current Depression was to boot out the politicians and replace them each year with whichever team won the World Series. We'd proclaimed that the humblest barbeque in Jerkwater, Kansas tasted better than the finest steak in Delmonico's Restaurant, never mind that neither of us had ever eaten a steak at Delmonico's or any other fine restaurant in New York City. And we'd pondered why the women we loved always broke our hearts and we kept coming back for more. It was the pondering over one woman in particular that had led me to the bottle, the barstool, and to bending the ear of my longtime pal and confidant, Tom, owner of the inn bearing his name.

Now it was late, the whiskey was gone, the inn was closed, and I was on the sidewalk, weaving on wobbly pins in front of a beat cop. I was filled to the gills with wisdom, wit, and bullet-proof courage. The cop was unimpressed.

"Okay, wise guy. Give me the keys. You're not driving anywhere."

. . .

Publisher: Meadowlark - 2020
ISBN: 978-1-7342477-3-2

Grandma was Special

Even before she told me her story about seeing the ghost of her great uncle, I knew my grandma was special. She possessed a quiet patience, a dignity sometimes lacking in others. When a crisis arose, when others flitted and flew and squandered time and energy on futile gestures, Grandma waited and observed. She bided her time, thoughtful and calm. She peered into corners and gazed into shadows. Grandma noticed things that other people missed.

"It was cold that night, cold and clear and still. An early frost hung in the air, and I tucked the blanket up under my chin. Full moon shining. What was it Papa said? A dying grass moon, he called it. That was it. A dying grass moon, that full October moon. Trees going bare, long shadows, no stars. Some claimed that spirits stirred on such a night. An owl hooted. A twig snapped. I started, my little girl imagination turning to ghosts and goblins and such. A body felt mighty small beneath that prairie sky."

"Were you scared, Grandma?"

"Oh, no, not really, not with Papa on one side and Momma on the other. I was safe. Our mare snorted and snuffed and leaned into the harness, blowing clouds of mist. The buggy creaked and rattled. I curled beneath the blanket and snuggled close to Momma. She slept on the seat, and her jowls jiggled as we passed over the rutted road. Papa dozed on my other side, reins loose over one hand. He'd snuck out behind the barn to tip a jug between dances, him and his pals, thinking the ladies would be none the wiser, and the ladies pretended they didn't notice. Corn liquor had lifted his spirits and claimed his body. He fought sleep. His head bobbed and dropped, down, down, then snapped up like a fish hooked on a line. He popped open his eyes, twisted his neck, puffed his cheeks and blew a breath. He gazed into the darkness, got his bearings and did it all over again. His eyelids drooped, his head bobbed, his chin dropped. I tried not to giggle. I wondered why he just didn't go to sleep. That mare knew the way home as well as Papa did, and she didn't need any prodding to get there neither."

Grandma's chuckle spilled over her pink gums, and her tongue flicked over her lips. Her teary eyes squinted behind the tiny wire-framed glasses that rested on her nose. Light from a dim bulb haloed the white bun atop her head. She looked angelic.

"What about the ghost, Grandma? When did you see the ghost?"

"Well, as we drew near our place the road rose up over a narrow bridge that passed over a creek. That was our guidepost, our signal that home was just ahead, that bridge. The mare knew it, too, and she leaned forward and stepped a bit faster. That's when I saw him, just out of the shadows, standing right there on that bridge in the light of the moon. I saw a tall man, a thin man, what we called gaunt. He wore long gray whiskers, and he had a black top hat. Under a dark coat he wore a red checkered vest with a gold chain draped across it."

"Wow, a real ghost! Now were you scared?"

Grandma smiled and gathered me in with fleshy arms and dimpled elbows and laid my head against her breast. She patted my head and whispered.

"No, child, no I wasn't afraid, not in the least . . ."

About the Author

Michael D. Graves created the character of Pete Stone as a memorial to his grandfather. The first and the third in the series were selected as Kansas Notable Books: *To Leave a Shadow* (2016) and *All Hallows' Shadows* (2021). *All Hallows' Shadows* was also the J. Donald Coffin Memorial Book Award winner by the Kansas Authors Club in 2020 and a silver medalist in the Midwest Book Awards in 2021.

Mike's writing has appeared in *Cheap Detective Stories, Thorny Locust, Flint Hills Review,* and elsewhere. He is an author of *Green Bike, a group novel,* along with Kevin Rabas and Tracy Million Simmons. He lives with his wife in Emporia, Kansas. They are both members of the Kansas Authors Club.

When life conjures its riddles, Mike turns to back roads and baseball for answers.

Acknowledgments

This is the fourth *Shadow* adventure, and many kind and generous people have assisted me along the way.

I'm grateful to Tracy Million Simmons and Evie Simmons of Meadowlark Press and to Dave Leiker of Dave Leiker Photography for working together to create another beautiful book. Tracy read early manuscripts and offered excellent editing suggestions. Dave created the artistic cover photographs. Evie was in charge of layout and design on books two and three. You continue to be the best team on the field. Thank you for working your magic.

My friend, Roger Heineken, is a writer and story-teller who brought the German American Bund to my attention. Roger shared articles and information that detailed activities of Bund members in the United States, and these prompted me to learn more about the organization's influence during the 1930s. Thank you, Roger.

Libraries and museums are important sources of information for my stories, and I'm grateful for the generosity of many people, including Michelle Enke at the Wichita Public Library and Jami Frazier Tracy at the Wichita Sedgwick County Historical Museum. The Kansas Historical Society museum and website have also been valuable resources.

Kansas Baseball 1858-1941, by Mark E. Eberle is a detailed study on the history of baseball in Kansas, including the 1934 construction of Lawrence (later Lawrence-Dumont) Stadium in Wichita. I met Mark several years ago at a book festival, and I'm pleased to own a copy of his excellent book. I refer to it often.

Kaye McIntyre of Kansas Public Radio is a dedicated and vocal supporter of many authors, and I'm thankful and pleased that Kaye has interviewed me on several occasions. She loves her work, and it shows. Kaye reads her authors' books, asks intelligent questions, and prepares entertaining and informative shows. Thank you, Kaye, for your support and friendship.

Thank you, also, to my friends and fellow writers in the Emporia Writers Group and the Kansas Authors Club for your on-going encouragement. Pete Stone and I wouldn't be here without your support.

Meadowlark
FICTION

Books are a way to explore, connect, and discover. Reading gives us the gift of living lives and gaining experiences beyond our own. Publishing books is our way of saying—

We love these words,
we want to play a role in preserving them,
and we want to help share them with the world.